FABLES

from

INCUNABULA

I0458158

to

MODERN PICTURE BOOKS

A Selective Bibliography

Compiled by

BARBARA QUINNAM

CHILDREN'S BOOK SECTION

General Reference and Bibliography Division : Reference Department

THE LIBRARY OF CONGRESS

Washington : 1966

L. C. Card 66–60012

COVER DESIGN: *Woodcut from Sir Thomas North's* The Morall Philosophie of Doni
(London, H. Denham, 1570). Court room scene. (Item 38)

For sale by the Superintendent of Documents, U.S. Government Printing Office
Washington, D.C., 20402 - Price 40 cents

FOREWORD

The rich holdings of fables in the Library, including the Rare Book Division's wealth in incunabula and other early editions, make the value of an exhibition of these volumes and illustrations immediately apparent. Among the incunabula, in particular, are 11 very rare items—8 Aesop and 3 Bidpai—which came to the Library in a munificent gift from Lessing J. Rosenwald. In a recent additional gift Mr. Rosenwald presented his set of Chagall prints for La Fontaine's fables. Items in the exhibit designated "Rosenwald Coll" are normally housed in the Alverthorpe Gallery in Jenkintown, Pennsylvania.

Within the broad and significant area that folklore has occupied through the years in literature for children, the importance of fables as animal tales is recognized by the Children's Book Section in its special concern for research in children's literature. Fables fall naturally among the briefest and simplest folktales shared with young children and have indeed been taken over as "Juvenile Classics."

A third reason for making fables the subject of an exhibition is the apparent compulsive delight with which great artists over the centuries have added their pictorial interpretations to written versions of fables. From the medieval woodcut to delicate engravings, and finally, to the bold, free line of Chagall, Calder, and Frasconi and the vibrant colors of Wildsmith, the range reveals the very history of book illustration.

In the exhibition and in the bibliography the items are arranged to show the lines of inheritance of this long-lived form of folklore. Built upon even more ancient oral literature, the written history of fables has encompassed many centuries. In remotest antiquity wise sayings were repeated, then drawn into stories of people and of animals representing human traits; each pointed a moral. Village storytellers included fables in their repertoires, and their tales were carried from place to place and from country to country. The title of Somadeva's *Kathā Sarit Sāgara,* or *Ocean of Streams of Story* (item 12), gives us the perfect picture of this line of influence. Here the author develops the idea of many streams flowing into the great body of literature and also of currents within the ocean carrying individual stories and motifs to widely separated parts of the world.

The lost Sanskrit original of the Panchatantra (or the Five Books) probably dates from somewhere between A.D. 100 and 500. This collection is composed of many older popular tales and has come down to us in two separate streams. Through the Pahlavi translation of the sixth century, it became the well-known *Kalīlah wa-Dimnah* in the Arabic version of Abdallāh ibn al-Moqaffa, made about 750. About 1250 it was translated into Latin by Giovanni da Capua as *Directorium Humanae Vitae* and from there it entered the German as *Buch der Beispiele* in the 15th century. The Italian of Doni in the 16th century was finally translated into English by Sir Thomas North in 1570 as *The Morall Philosophie of Doni*. The second stream branched off from the Arabic *Kalilah wa-Dimnah* in the early 12th century and became *Anvār-i Suhailī* in an old Persian translation of Nosrallah. Another Persian version, *Anwār-i-Suhalī* by Husain ibn Ali-al-Wa'iz, appeared in the 15th century and was the source for the French *Livre des Lumières*, later known as the *Fables de Pilpay* or *Bidpai*. Separate from the two main streams is the Hitopadeśa, tales collected by Nārāyana from the Panchatantra and other sources.

Aesop, the shadowy, almost mythical figure of antiquity, wrote nothing himself. The earliest-known written versions of fables associated with his name are those of Phaedrus, who lived in the first century A.D. and wrote 200 fables in Latin meter, and the Greek verse collection (some 300 fables) of Babrius, who lived in the early third century A.D. Avianus in the 4th century and Romulus in the 10th century added to the early body of fable literature. The collection made by Romulus is essentially a prose rendering of Phaedrus, with some additions.

Well known as an example of a fable that traveled down the years to La Fontaine and more modern retellers is "La Laitière et le pot au lait," or "The Maid and the Spilt Milk." The tale appears in the D'Aulaires' picture-story book as "Don't Count Your Chicks." Professor Max Müller, who in his essay "On the Migration of Fables" item 1) has traced the travels of this fable from the Panchatantra and the Hitopadeśa through the Arabic and many versions of the 11th, 12th, and 13th centuries, has concluded that La Fontaine must have derived his idea from some version of the medieval collection, *Dialogus Creaturarum Moralisatus*. In the older versions there is, instead of Perrette the young milkmaid, a Brahman; and instead of milk, it is grain that is spilt.

In general, the editions listed here are collections of fables which clearly show a derivation from early folklore. Omitted thus are the works of such authors as John Gay, Tomás de Iriarte, and Gotthold Lessing, who made literary use of the fable form, and the well-known *Fables for Our Times* of James Thurber. Also omitted (except for one juvenile collection) are the broad, general, world-wide fable anthologies such as those compiled by Manuel Komroff in *The Great Fables* (New York, Dial Press, 1928) and Frederic Taber Cooper in *Argosy of Fables* (New York, Stokes, 1921). Facsimiles and reprints are not included unless accompanied by extensive and important notes or introductions.

Scholars contributing to a vast literature on the fable have devoted years to careful, detailed analysis, commentary, and reconstruction. This selective bibliography little more than touches upon the results of their scholarship.

Consideration of the dissemination and variants of fables, as for any form of folklore, offers both the scientific folklorist and the student of literature a wide field for research and enjoyment. Here in display and bibliography, fables offer a particular reward in the study of migration and inheritance of folklore.

VIRGINIA HAVILAND
Head, Children's Book Section

CONTENTS

KEY TO SYMBOLS

Batchelder Coll—Batchelder Collection, Rare Book Division

Min Case   —Miniature Case, Rare Book Division

NNUW   —Washington Square Library, New York University Libraries

OCl   —Cleveland Public Library

Orien Arab   —Orientalia Division, Arabic Section

Rare Bk   —Rare Book Division, Library of Congress

Rosenwald Coll—Rosenwald Collection, Rare Book Division

Thacher Coll   —Thacher Collection, Rare Book Division

Vollbehr Coll   —Vollbehr Collection, Rare Book Division

Yudin Coll   —Yudin Collection, Rare Book Division

☆   —Indicates item on exhibit

Woodcut from Vita *et Aesopus Moralisatus* (*Naples, Francesco del Tuppo, 1485*).
(*Item 62*)

GENERAL STUDIES

1 Müller, F. Max. ON THE MIGRATION OF FABLES. *In* Library of the world's best literature, edited by Charles Dudley Warner. v. 18. New York, J. A. Hill [c1902] p. 10429–10441. PN6013.W3, v. 18

Professor Müller follows the fable of "The Maid and Her Pail of Milk" from its beginnings to the well-known version by La Fontaine, who admits that the idea for it came from Pilpay. His careful study traces the story from the Panchatantra, to the Hitopadeśa, to the Arabic translation in *Kalīlah wa-Dimnah,* and to the version of Symeon, son of Seth (about 1080); he mentions the many versions published in the 11th, 12th, and 13th centuries, notes the fable's use by Rabelais in *Gargantua,* and finally concludes that it must have come to La Fontaine from some version of the *Dialogus Creaturarum Moralisatus,* a medieval collection of beast tales.

A masterful condensation of a great mass of material, using an interesting example.

2 Aesopus. AESOP; five centuries of illustrated fables. Selected by John J. McKendry. New York, Metropolitan Museum of Art; distributed by New York Graphic Society, 1964. 95 p. PA3855.E5M27

☆ Produced in connection with an exhibit at the museum, this study shows the great variety of styles in illustration for the fables. Those reproduced range from 15th-century German and Italian woodcuts to the works of two contemporary artists, Antonio Frasconi and Joseph Low. Each of the 40 illustrations has been matched with a more or less contemporaneous translation by writers ranging from William Caxton to Marianne Moore. The comments and brief historical outline in Mr. McKendry's introduction are succinct and enlightening.

Indian and Related Fables

INDIAN AND RELATED FABLES

The Panchatantra

Rivaling Aesop in antiquity, although not so well known in the West, is a collection of fables from India called the Panchatantra (Five Books, or in Sanskrit, Five Threads). In it Vishnu Sarma undertakes to teach the three unruly sons of the king the principles of conduct befitting them as princes. He tells them five series of stories on the topics the Loss of Friends; the Winning of Friends; the War Between the Crows and Owls; Loss of Gains; and Ill-Considered Action. The five frame stories include 32 "emboxed" stories, which were probably popular folktales and fables of unknown age. The fables are in prose, with aphoristic verses interspersed.

The earliest Sanskrit manuscript of the Panchatantra, the *Tantrākhyāyika*, dates from somewhere between 275 B.C. and A.D. 275. In the sixth century A.D. the Panchatantra was translated into Pahlavi by the physician Burzuyeh (Burzoë) under the patronage of the Persian monarch Chosrau Anūshīrwān (Chosros I). From this a translation was made into Syriac in A.D. 570, and into Arabic about 750. In the 13th century it was translated into Latin as *Directorum Humanae Vitae* by Giovanni da Capua, whose version influenced Boccaccio, La Fontaine, and many others. Among the earliest printed books are collections of Aesopic fables and Bidpai fables, in Latin, German (*Buch der Weishait*), Spanish (*Exemplario contra los engaños*), and Italian. From the Italian version of Doni, *La Moral Filosophia*, published in 1552, Sir Thomas North translated the first version in English, *The Morall Philosophie of Doni*, in 1570. (See the note on Bidpai.)

Franklin Edgerton, who has reconstructed the Panchatantra from various manuscripts, comments on its popularity: "Some idea of the enormous spread of the *Pañchatantra* can be obtained from the fact that there are known to exist over two hundred different versions in over fifty languages. It reached Europe in the eleventh century, and before 1600 existed in Greek, Latin, Spanish, Italian, German, English, Old Slavonic and Czech."—*Ocean of Story* (item 12), v. 5, appendix 1, p. 207

HERTEL STUDIES

3 Hertel, Johannes. DAS PAÑCATANTRA, seine geschichte und seine verbreitung. Leipzig, B. G. Teubner, 1914. xviii, [460] p.

PK3741.P4H4

It is upon the work of this German authority that all later studies of the Panchatantra are based. He concludes that there were two independent streams of Panchatantra tradition: *Tantrākhyāyika* and "K," archetype of all other versions, and that these go back to an archetype which he calls "T." He assumes also an intermediate archetype "N–W," to which may be traced the Southern Panchatantra (and its relatives, the Nepalese Panchatantra and the Hitopadeśa), the Pahlavi, and the Simplicior.

Hertel discusses in detail the many versions and recensions and develops a genealogical table which includes all the known versions as well as his conjectured ones. Items 4–8 are earlier studies which support Hertel's conclusions in this work.

Tantrākhyāyika

This recension is most important, as it has been estimated to contain 95 percent of the original text, besides a considerable amount of material not in the original. The manuscript, discovered by Hertel, came from Kashmir. He considered it "the only version which contains the unabbreviated and not intentionally altered language of the author."

4   Panchatantra. UBER DAS TANTRĀKHYĀYIKA, die kaśmirische rezension des Pancatantra. Mit dem texte der handschrift Decc. coll. VIII, 145. Von Johannes Hertel. Leipzig, B. G. Teubner, 1904. 154 p. plates.   PK3741.P2   1904

5   —— TANTRĀKHYĀYIKA. Die älteste fassung des Pancatantra. Aus dem sanskrit übersetzt mit einleitung und anmerkungen von Johannes Hertel. Leipzig, B. G. Teubner, 1909. 2 v. diagr.
                                                           PK3741.P3G4   1909

Southern Panchatantra

6   Hertel, Johannes. DAS SÜDLICHE PANCATANTRA, übersicht über den inhalt der alteren "Pancatantra"—rezensionen bis auf Pürnabhadra. Leipzig, F. A. Brockhaus, 1904. 68 p.   OCl

Another version edited by Hertel, characteristic of southern India. One subrecension is much like the *Tantrākhyāyika*, and in some cases bears even a closer resemblance to the original. A related offshoot of this version is the Nepalese. The well-known Hitopadeśa is still another version derived from the same text as the Nepalese. In both these versions books 1 and 2 of the Panchatantra are transposed and the rest of the work has been entirely remodeled and augmented, the whole containing four books instead of five. Book 3 has a frame story which bears little resemblance to that in book 3 of the Panchatantra while that in book 4 is new. The frame and substories of book 5 of the Panchatantra, as well as several others from books 1 and

6

3, appear in books 3 and 4 of these versions. Several stories are omitted from the Hitopadeśa and others are substituted from other works used by Nārāyana. The Hitopadeśa contains over half the substories of the Panchatantra.

The Pahlavi Version

The Pahlavi version is one of the oldest known and must have been translated from a very ancient Sanskrit text. Its descendants have become familiar to us under such names as Bidpai, the *Fables of Pilpay, Kalīlah wa-Dimnah, Lights of Canopus,* and *The Morall Philosophie of Doni.* They are described in the section on Bidpai.

The Jain Versions

Textus Simplicior is the name applied by its first modern editor to a version written by a Jaina monk between A.D. 900 and 1199. It has the same archetype as the *Tantrākhyāyika.*

Purnabhadra, also a Jaina monk, composed another version of the Panchatantra in A.D. 1199, drawing his text for the first two books mainly from the *Tantrākhyāyika* and for the last three mainly from the *Simplicior.*

7 Panchatantra. THE PANCHATANTRA; a collection of ancient Hindu tales in the recension, called Panchakhyanaka, and dated 1199 A.D., of the Jaina monk, Purnabhadra, critically edited in the original Sanskrit by Dr. Johannes Hertel. Cambridge, Mass., Harvard University, 1908. xlviii, 298 p. 2 double facsims. (Harvard oriental series, v. 11)   PK2971.H3, v. 11

8 ―― THE PANCHATANTRA-TEXT OF PURNABHADRA and its relation to texts of allied recensions as shown in parallel specimens, by Dr. Johannes Hertel. Cambridge, Mass., Harvard University, 1912. x p., 38 fold. 1. 26½ cm. (Harvard oriental series, v. 13)
PK2971.H3, v. 13

OTHER TEXTS AND STUDIES

9 Panchatantra. PANTSCHATANTRA: FÜNF BÜCHER INDISCHER FAB- ELN, MÄRCHEN UND ERZÄHLUNGEN. Aus dem Sanskrit übers. mit einleitung und anmerkungen von Theodor Benfey. Leipzig, F. A. Brockhaus, 1859. 2 v. (611, 556 p.)   PK3741.P3G4

Benfey was the first modern German translator of the Panchatantra. "His Introduction to his Translation, made him the founder of the comparative history of literature. Here he examined, with extraordinary acuteness, the migrations of Indian stories in the various languages of the East and West throughout the world."—Alfred Williams in *Tales From the Pañchatantra* (item 14)

7

In volume 1 Benfey compares the relation of the Panchatantra to the mythologies of other countries and to the traditional literature of the West such as Aesop and the Reynard stories. Volume 2 contains the translation and notes.

10 Brown, William N. THE PAÑCATANTRA IN MODERN INDIAN FOLK-LORE. Part 1, including the story themes of Pañcatantra, book 1, with an appendix: bibliography of Indian folktales. New Haven, 1919. 54 p. PK3647.B8

Thesis (Ph. D.), Johns Hopkins University, 1916; printed in the *Journal of the American Oriental Society*, v. 39. A study which compares 17 stories from book 1 of the older versions of the Panchatantra with the same stories from oral sources, as given in many collections of Indian folktales. The valuable 10-page bibliography gives critical notes on the various collections used for comparison.

11 Panchatantra. THE PANCHATANTRA RECONSTRUCTED; an attempt to establish the lost original Sanskrit text of the most famous of Indian story-collections on the basis of the principal extant versions; text, critical apparatus, introduction, translation, by Franklin Edgerton. New Haven, American Oriental Society, 1924. 2 v. (409, 405 p.) (American Oriental series, v. 2–3) PK3741.P2 1924

Volume 1 contains the transliterated Sanskrit text which Edgerton considers the closest approach to the original text of the Panchatantra, with a "Critical Apparatus" containing the evidence for this reconstructed text, sentence by sentence and verse by verse.

In volume 2 the author establishes four independent streams of Panchatantra tradition: (1) Tantrākhyāyika, Simplicior, and Purnabhadra; (2) Southern Panchatantra, Nepalese Panchatantra, and Hitopadeśa; (3) the Brhathatha versions, Somadeva and Ksemendra; and (4) the Pahlavi versions. All of these point to a definite literary archetype—an original Panchatantra—which the editor reconstructs by taking the parts common to all.

Chapter 5 of the second volume is a critical analysis of Hertel's views of the interrelationships of the versions and his hypothesis of a lost version and two secondary archetypes (see item 3). Edgerton refutes all of Hertel's arguments. Chapters 6 and 7 demonstrate, through examples and following the process step by step, how Edgerton reconstructed the text. Pages 190–258 include a conspectus of text-units and an elaborate table showing how the versions correspond with the reconstruction. Pages 274–405 contain his translation of this reconstruction of the original Panchatantra.

12 Somadeva Bhatta. THE OCEAN OF STORY, being C. H. Tawney's translation of Somadeva's Kathā sarit sāgara (or Ocean of streams of story) now edited with introduction, fresh explanatory notes and terminal essay, by N. M. Penzer. v. 5. London, Privately printed for

subscribers only by C. J. Sawyer, 1924.   324 p.   PK3741.S7E5   1924

The Panchatantra is included in this volume of the 10-volume set, in its place in Somadeva Bhatta's great collection of Indian stories dating from the 11th century.

The foreword by E. Denison Ross reports the results of his original research into the Persian and Arabic recensions of the Panchatantra, *Kalilah wa-Dimnah.* "The legend about this Old Persian compilation has been handed down by a number of early Arabic writers, beginning in the eighth century with the translator Ibnu 'l-Muqaffa himself, and has been retold in a famous passage in Firdawsi's Shahnama" (p. v). He examines in detail the Burzoë legend and presents a new theory which discounts the existence of the early Pahlavi version, as hypothesized by Benfey, Nöldecke, and others.

Appendix I, p. 207–242, gives an excellent résumé of the history and various recensions of the Panchatantra based mainly on the work of Hertel and Edgerton. The elaborate genealogical table of the Panchatantra prepared by Edgerton is included, with his notes of explanation.

13   Panchatantra. *English.* THE PANCHATANTRA, translated from the Sanskrit by Arthur W. Ryder. Chicago, University of Chicago Press [c1925] 470 p.   PK3741.P3E5   1925a

The complete five books of wise and witty fables—"The Loss of Friends"; "The Winning of Friends"; "Crows and Owls"; "Loss of Gains"; "Ill-Considered Action"—make up this textbook on the "art of intelligent living" or conduct of life. It keeps the frame stories for each book and the stories within stories, the verses being translated as verse.

Animal names appear in English as "Lively" (the bull), "Rusty" (the lion), and "Cheek" and "Victor" (the jackals). Except for this awkward use of English equivalents for the animals' names, the work is a pleasant and idiomatic translation, in which the reader is made aware of the Indian background and religious outlook. As the translator says, it was made "to extend accurate and joyful acquaintance with one of the world's masterpieces."

14   ——— TALES FROM THE PANCHATANTRA, translated from the Sanskrit by Alfred Williams; illustrated by Peggy Whistler; with an introductory note by A. A. Macdonell. Oxford, B. Blackwell, 1930. 207 p.
                                           PK3741.P3E5   1930

☆   Because the arrangement of the "emboxed" stories within the frame stories might be confusing to English readers, the translator has detached each fable from its frame story, dropped unnecessary stanzas, and presented each story complete in itself. He has retold 67 of them gracefully and naturally, but one misses the frame stories.

15 Panchapakesa Ayyar, Aiylam S., *ed. and tr.* PANCHATANTRA AND HITOPADEŚA STORIES; translation and introduction. Bombay, D. B. Taraporevala Sons [c1931] 219 p. (Great short stories of India [v. 1]) PK3741.P3E5 1931

Omitting the first and third frame stories and the introductory chapter, the editor retells 45 separate stories from the Panchatantra, plus 4 from the Hitopadeśa. An elaborate and involved introduction in Anglo-Indian style explains the background and meaning of the subjects, the use of the frame stories, and the various characters in the stories, with comments on each story. Footnotes give the meanings of the Indian names for the animals.

16 Panchatantra, *German.* PANTSCHATANTRA. [Aus dem Sanskrit über-tragen von Theodor Benfey. Zusammengestellt und sprachlich bearbeitet von Friedmar Geissler. Mit Nachworten von Walter Ruben und Friedmar Geissler.] Berlin, Rütten & Loening [1962] 336 p. PK3741.P3G4 1962

☆ This charming modern German edition uses the translation of Theodor Benfey. It is decorated with small drawings by Bert Heller in black and lavender on the margins of every page.

EDITIONS FOR CHILDREN

17 Panchatantra. *English.* ANCIENT INDIAN FABLES AND STORIES, being a selection from the Panchatantra, by Stanley Rice. New York, E. P. Dutton, 1924. 126 p. (Wisdom of the East)

PK3741.P3E5 1924a

In his brief preface the author states that this selection is retold, not actually translated, from the version from southern India, since it is older than the extant Sanskrit edition and has been less exposed to outside influences.

These selections preserve the frame stories as well as many of the fables in a graceful although condensed version, keeping the Indian names for the animals.

18 ——— GOLD'S GLOOM; tales from the Panchatantra, translated by Arthur W. Ryder. Chicago, University of Chicago Press [c1925] [152] p. PK3741.P3E5 1925

Thirty-four of the stories from Ryder's translation (item 13) of the five books of the Panchatantra, but with the "frame" arrangement usually ignored and the stories told separately and in random order.

The Hitopadeśa

The Hitopadeśa, or Book of Good Counsels, is a rearrangement of much of the Panchatantra, with additions from other sources. The collection, made by Nārāyana, dates from about the 10th century A.D. It contains only four books, with four frame stories, and more than half the substories of the Panchatantra, with the first two books transposed. Stories from the remaining three books of the Panchatantra are incorporated at different places throughout the text of books 3 and 4 of the Hitopadeśa. The frame stories are "The Four Friends: Crow, Rat, Deer, and Tortoise"; "Kalilah and Dimnah"; "Crows and Owls"; and "The Monkey and the Crocodile."

TEXTS AND STUDIES

19 Hitopadeśa. THE HITOPADEŚA IN THE SANSKRITA LANGUAGE. [Edited by A. Hamilton] London, Library, East-India House: Cox, Son, and Baylis, Printers, 1810. 119 p. PK3741.H5 1810

☆ Advertised as "the first *Sanskrit* book ever printed in Europe," this was prepared as a class book for a college in Calcutta. It was based on an 1804 Calcutta edition edited by H. T. Colebrook. The copy exhibited has been decorated by an unknown user.

20 Hitopadeśa. *English*. HITOPADEŚA; or salutary counsels of Vishnu Sarman; in a series of connected fables, interspersed with moral, prudential, and political maxims. Translated from the Sanskrit, by Francis Johnson. Hertford, S. Austin, 1848. 121 p.
PK3741.H6E5 1848

The translator intended to help the student of Sanskrit "to render his knowledge of the whole work more easy of attainment . . . not so much to give it the adaptation which justice to the literary merits of the original would require, as to express the sense with as close a conformity to the Sanskrit as it was possible for the English language to adopt."

Although the arrangement in 136 numbered verses made it difficult to follow the narrative, the work was useful as a classbook and as a basis for later versions. Lionel Barnett in 1928 (item 23) says that Francis Johnson's translation of the Hitopadeśa was a remarkable piece of work, considering the condition of Sanskrit studies in 1848.

21 —— FABLES AND PROVERBS FROM THE SANSKRIT, being the Hitopadesa translated by Charles Wilkins. With an introduction by Henry Morley. 2d ed. London, New York, G. Routledge, 1886. 277 p.
PK3741.H6E5 1886

A translation that contains all of the fables within fables, first published in 1787, with a translator's preface giving the history of the Hitopadeśa and its versions in Persian (Kalīlah wa-Dimnah), in French (Pilpay), English (Bidpai), and Turkish. The proverbs are translated in prose. The introduction relates the Hitopadeśa to the Vedic literature and the Upanishads.

As Wilkins said in the preface, "In 1709 the Kulila Dumna, the Persian version of Abul Mala Nasser Alla Mustofi made in the 515th year of the Hegira, was translated into French with the title *Les Conseils et les Maximes de Pilpay, Philosophe Indien.* . . . This edition resembles the Hitopadesa more than any other I have seen, and is evidently the immediate original of the English."

22   Hitopadeśa. HITOPADESA BY NÂRÂYANA. Edited by Peter Peterson. Bombay, Government Central Book Depôt, 1887. 63, 161, 96 p.

PK3741.H5 1887

According to the editor's preface "this edition of the Hitopadeśa was prepared originally from three manuscripts belonging to the Collection of the Government of Bombay." To these was added a fourth, from the British Museum, which is the oldest one known, dating from 1373.

Peterson retells the Hitopadeśa (p. 1–63) and then prints the text in Sanskrit, with footnotes listing the variants in the four manuscripts. He provides 87 pages of notes and an index of the first lines of the Sanskrit and points out Jātaka sources for many of the stories.

23   Hitopadeśa. *English.* HITOPADEŚA, THE BOOK OF WHOLESOME COUNSEL; a translation from the original Sanskrit by Francis Johnson. Revised and in part re-written, with an introduction by Lionel D. Barnett. With a frontispiece by Cynthia Kent. London, Chapman and Hall, 1928. 201 p. (The treasure house of Eastern story)

PK3741.H6E5 1928

☆   Lionel Barnett, in his introduction, gives a brief history of the Hitopadeśa and shows its relationship to the Panchatantra. Although he has based his translation on Francis Johnson's of 1848 (item 20), he has "revised, recast, and in many places entirely rewritten [Johnson's] translation, on the basis of the text published by him, with the utmost care . . . and added short notes wherever they were needful. The verses in the text [are] printed in italics. The present book is therefore almost a new version." It is much more readable than Johnson's, because of its format and typography as well as the clearer translation.

24   Sternbach, Ludwik. THE HITOPADEŚA AND ITS SOURCES. New Haven, American Oriental Society, 1960. 109 p. (American Oriental series, v. 44)

PK3741.H7S75

In this study the author concludes that "of 71 motifs of tales, 56 can be traced to the Pañcatantra while of 786 stanzas found in all editions of the Hitopadeśa in question, more than 70 percent were borrowed from other sources of Sanskrit literature, or were directly affected by these sources. . . . About 20 percent of motifs and about 30 percent of the poetical part of the Hitopadeśa seem to be original." Six tables show in detail, line by line, the correlation between Hitopadeśa, and Panchatantra tales and stanzas, and between Hitopadeśa

One day a hermit
sat thinking about
big and little—
Suddenly,
he saw a mouse

Woodcut by Marcia Brown for Once a Mouse, *a picture book based on a story from the Hitopadeśa. Copyright © 1961 Marcia Brown; reproduced with the permission of Charles Scribner's Sons. (Item 25)*

stanzas and Niti-śastras, Canakya's aphorisms, Dharna śastras, and the Epics, Puranas, Kātha, Kanya, and other literary works. Nārāyana, the author of the Hitopadeśa, was "a great compiler and an excellent writer and this is where his actual greatness lies" (p. 20).

CHILDREN'S EDITION

25 Hitopadeśa. *English. Selections.* ONCE A MOUSE. A fable cut in wood by Marcia Brown. New York, Scribner [1961] [32] p. 25 cm.
PZ8.2.H5On

☆ The story of the saint and the mouse is fable 6 in book 4 of the Hitopadeśa. Bold woodcuts in two shades of green and dull red give distinction to this concise storyteller's version.

The Jātakas

The collection of about 550 stories entitled "Jātaka" or "The Jātakas" is included in the second of the threefold Pali (Buddhist) Canon, known as the Pitakas. The stories of the Buddha's former births, or "Tales of the Past," are the parts that have become familiar as fables in the West. Some of the same stories are included in the Sanskrit Panchatantra, Hitopadeśa, and their descendants.

The Jātakas are not arranged within frame stories as are the Hindu collections. Each one is separate with its own location and setting, told as a remembered happening in a former incarnation of the Buddha, brought to mind by a particular saying or event in the present, the "Tale of the Present." The "Tale of the Past" is always told as though Buddha himself were speaking. One of the actors in the story, often the weaker of the animals or people, but the most kind, or clever, or thoughtful, turns out to be the Bodhisat. "The Banyan deer was just I."

TEXTS AND STUDIES

26 Jātakas. BUDDHIST BIRTH STORIES; OR, JĀTAKA TALES. The oldest collection of folk-lore extant: being the Jātakatthavaṇṇanā, for the first time edited in the original Pāli by V. Fausböll, and translated by T. W. Rhys Davids. v. 1. London, Trübner, 1880. ciii, 347 p. (Trübner's oriental series)   BL1411.J3E5   1880a

    The first volume of this projected translation includes only 40 stories, but preceding them are the translator's history and background of the birth stories (p. i–ciii) and his long introductory "talk" (p. 1–133), entitled Nidānakathā, "Talk on the Origin," or "Causes That Lead to the Attainment of Buddhahood." This was the only volume published by Rhys Davids; he handed the work over to the eminent Indologist Edward Cowell, who, with a group of workers, published the complete translation from 1897 to 1907 (Cambridge [Eng.] University Press) in 6 volumes.

    The Danish scholar M. Viggo Fausböll published his edition, in Roman letters, of the original Pali (London, Trübner, 1875–97).

27 ——— THE JĀTAKA; or Stories of the Buddha's former births. Translated from the Pāli by various hands under the editorship of Professor E. B. Cowell. Cambridge [Eng.] University Press, 1895–1907. 6 v.   BL1411.J3E4

    The complete translation of the Pali text edited by Fausböll was the result of the work of four other scholars and Edward B. Cowell himself, who translated part of the sixth volume. The others were Robert Chalmers, W. H. D. Rouse, H. T. Francis, and R. A. Neil. A 63-page index was published in 1913.

28 Jātakas. JATAKA TALES RE-TOLD by Ellen C. Babbitt; with illustra-
☆ tions by Ellsworth Young. New York, Century, 1912. 92 p.
PZ10.3.J36Jar

29 ——— MORE JATAKA TALES RETOLD by Ellen C. Babbitt, with illustrations by Ellsworth Young. New York, Century, 1922. 92 p.
PZ10.3.J36Mor

☆ Taken from the complete edition of the Jātaka edited by E. B.
Cowell (item 27), these are excellent versions for younger children.
They are true to the original, and the clear, simple style preserves the
humor which makes them popular with young children. The names
of plants and animals are sometimes changed from strange to more
familiar ones. Small silhouettes illustrate the 18 tales in the first
volume, 21 in *More Jataka Tales*.

30 Shedlock, Marie L. EASTERN STORIES AND LEGENDS. Foreword by
Prof. T. W. Rhys Davids; introduction by Annie Carroll Moore. New
York, E. P. Dutton [c1920] 212 p. PZ8.1.S538Ea

One of the earliest collections of Jātaka tales for children, these 30
stories retold by the famous storyteller retain the catchword or briefly
stated lesson at the beginning of each tale to show the connection with
Buddha. They are based on the translations from the Pali made by
T. W. Rhys Davids. Notes, p. 203–212, give hints for application of
the stories. An edition better suited to older children.

Eloise Ramsey in *Folklore for Children and Young People* (Philadelphia, American Folklore Society, 1952), ranks this as "the best
selection from the Jātakas for young people we have had in English."

31 Jātakas. JATAKA TALES OUT OF OLD INDIA, retold by Marguerite As-
pinwall, with illustrations by Arnold Hall. New York, Putnam, 1927.
239 p. PZ10.3.J36Ja

These tales, retold more simply for children, were taken from the
collection of Jātakas selected and edited by H. T. Francis and E. J.
Thomas, published by Cambridge University Press.

"Once upon a time Brahmadatta was king in Benares," the stories
begin, giving the time and setting. The *gāthas*, the canonical stanzas
included in each tale, are translated in verse, as in the original. Here
is a different selection; although some tales are also in Babbitt and
some in Shedlock, others are new. Many of the stories come from the
Hitopadeśa. More of these stories tell of people, although many tell
of animals, too. Some seem rather gory or grim, but justice is always
satisfied.

32 ——— STORIES OF THE BUDDHA, being selections from the Jātaka,
with an introduction by Mrs. Rhys Davids. London, Chapman and

Hall, 1929. xxvii, 244 p. (The Treasure house of Eastern story)

BL1411.J3E47   1929

The wife of the English oriental scholar selected these 47 of the stories of former births of the Buddha from about 550 in the full collection.   For her translation she kept as close as possible to the original Pali.   She gives the setting and "Tale of the Present" for each Jātaka as well as the "Tale of the Past."

Her introduction gives the Buddhist background and emphasizes the importance of keeping in mind the Way of Buddhism in interpreting these stories.   Mrs. Rhys Davids believed herself to be a reincarnation of the chief female disciple of the Buddha.   The Jātaka collection was continually growing and changing until it was written down "somewhere about the beginning of our era"; thus it is now "like a great petrified tree."

33 ——— Twenty Jataka tales.   Retold by Noor Inayat and pictured by H. Willebeek Le Mair.   Philadelphia, David McKay [c1939] 138 p.   PZ10.3.J36Tw2

☆   These tales are selected from the *Gataka-mala,* or *Garland of Birth-Stories,* by Ayre Sûra, translated from the Sanskrit by J. S. Speyer (Oxford University Press), and *The Jataka; or Stories of the Buddha's Former Births* (item 27), translated from the Pali.   The telling has a familiar easy style, more ornate than Babbitt's, with a fitting oriental setting and a strongly underlying Buddhist philosophy.   Willebeek Le Mair's delicate drawings illustrate almost every story.

Bidpai

Bidpai has been called the Indian Aesop, and his real identity is as obscure as the Greek fabulist's.   According to Silvestre de Sacy, Bidpai (pronounced Bidbai) signifies "lecteur du Veda, étant formé du mot ved ou veda . . . et de vajana, lecture."   As the Persians call the Brahmans *lecteurs du véda,* the form Bidpai may be a corruption of the Sanskrit *vidva* (Wise Man), the title given to Vishnu Sarma, who was a Brahman.

The body of literature associated with the name Bidpai has two main versions, both from the Pahlavi version: the Arabic *Kalīlah wa-Dimnah* and the Persian *Anvār-i Suhailī.*   In A.D. 531 Anushirwan, or Noshirwan, had become King of Persia.   He was known among the Arabs as Kisra, and as Chosroes I by Western writers.   A Sanskrit manuscript of the Panchatantra came into the King's hands, who gave it to a court physician named Burzoë or Burzuyeh to be translated into Pahlavi, then the official language of Persia.   Burzoë titled his translation after the two jackals, Karataka and Damanaka, who appear in the first book, whence the Arabic *Kalīlah wa-Dimnah.*   The Arabic translation, the work of Abdallāh ibn al-Moqaffa, who was executed about 750, became very popular and many adaptations and other translations soon came into being.   The oldest of them is probably one in Syriac of the 10th century. This was edited by Wright in 1884 and is familiar through Keith-Falconer's translation at Cambridge in 1885 (item 43).

The Persian version made by Naṣr Allah in 1121 is important because from it came the better-known Persian version, *Anvār-i Suhailī,* which was translated into numerous European languages and became known in England as the *Lights of Canopus* through the translations of Eastwick in 1854 and Wollaston in 1877 and 1894. French editions came mostly to be called *Fables de Pilpay* and were frequently translated into English. The second part of *Anvār-i Suhailī* is concerned with the trial and punishment of Dimnah. It is not found in the Sanskrit and was apparently invented by an author who did not want to see such treachery go unpunished.

The Hebrew version composed in the 12th or 13th century was the basis of the famous Latin version of Giovanni da Capua—*Directorium Humanae Vitae*—which contributed so largely to the spread of oriental stories in Europe. It first appeared in Germany in 1480 as *Buch der Beispiele der alten Weisen,* by Anthonius von Pfor (or Pforr).

The fables became popular also in Spain. A Spanish translation formed the basis of Firenzuola's *Discorsi degli Animali* (16 editions between 1648 and 1895). Directly built on the Latin version was the work of the Italian Doni, which appeared under the title of *La Moral Filosophia,* and from this came Sir Thomas North's English version, *The Morall Philosophie of Doni,* 1570. The edition of 1888, issued by David Nutt, contains an introduction and "Pedigree of the Bidpai Literature," by Joseph Jacobs.

Bidpai also reappears in *Reynard the Fox,* a beast epic which grew up in Europe in the Middle Ages. The structure of the frame story is similar to the court setting in *Anvār-i Suhailī,* with Reynard the accused instead of Dimnah, although for different reasons. The substitution of the fox for the jackal is usual in the transfer of folklore from the East to the West.

KALĪLAH WA-DIMNAH

Incunabula

34 Bidpai. *Arabic version. Kalīlah wa-Dimnah. German.* DIRECTO-
RIUM HUMANAE VITAE. German. Ulm, Lienhart Holle, May 28, 1483.
[196] l., the last blank. fol. 29.5 cm.

Incun. 1483.B57 Rosenwald Coll

☆ Leaf [195ᵃ] gives the title in German: *Hier endet sich das Buch der Weishait, der alten Weisen von Anbeginne der Welt von Geschlecht zu Geschlecht.* It was also known as *Buch der Beispiele der alten Weisen.*

This early German translation by Anthonius von Pforr (or Pfor) from the Latin of Giovanni da Capua is beautifully printed in Gothic type with initials supplied in red. The woodcuts are large with clearly outlined figures. This copy is preserved in the original binding with part of the clasps still attached.

Woodcut from Buch der Weishait (*Ulm, Lienhart Holle, 1483*). *The Lion already regrets killing his friend the Bull.* (*Item 34*)

35   Bidpai. *Arabic version. Kalīlah wa-Dimnah. Latin.* DIRECTORIUM HUMANAE VITAE. [Strassburg, Johann Prüss, ca. 1488–93. 82] l. fol. 27.5 cm.   Incun. X.B567

☆   The first leaf contains the complete title: *Directorium Humanae Vitae Alias Parabole Antiquorū Sapientū.*

    In this Latin version of Giovanni da Capua appear 119 curious, primitive woodcuts—the Lion with his flowing mane and the jackals strangely resembling monkeys. Large initials, paragraph marks, and initial strokes are added in red to the neat Gothic type.

36 Bidpai. *Arabic version. Kalīlah wa-Dimnah. Spanish.* DIRECTORIUM HUMANAE VITAE. Spanish. Zaragoza, Paul Hurus, 15 April 1494. [i], ii–cvi (i.e. 103), [1] l., the last, probably blank, wanting. fol. 28.5 cm.
Incun. 1494.B53   Rosenwald Coll

☆   The first leaf has a woodcut containing the title: *Exemplario contra los engaños: y peligros del mūdo.*

Anonymous translations from the Latin version of Giovanni da Capua.

A complete and unique copy of the second edition, the only complete Spanish edition printed in the 15th century that is known. (The first edition, of 1493, exists as only a fragment in Madrid.) The large, primitive woodcuts, of bold design and good proportion, are the same as those in the Johann Prüss edition of 1488–93, with Spanish borders added.   There are also decorated initials.

Woodcut from Exemplario contra los engaños (*Zaragoza, Paul Hurus, 1494*). *The Tortoise and the Geese. (Item 36)*

37 Bidpai. *Arabic version. Kalīlah wa-Dimnah. Italian. Doni. 1552.*
LA MORAL FILOSOPHIA DEL DONI, tratta da gli antichi scrittori. Vinegia,
F. Marcolini, 1552. 152, 103 p. 21 cm.

PN989.15M45 1552 Rosenwald Coll

☆   This volume is divided into three books with halftitles for books
2 and 3 reading "della filosophia de sapienti antichi . . . scritto de
Sendebar" and "Trattati diversi de Sendebar" and bearing the im-
print: Nell 'Academia Peregrina. The whole is a translation by the
members of the Academia dei Pellegrini from Giovanni da Capua's
Latin version of Bidpai's fables and is edited by Antonio Francesco
Doni.

The woodcuts are in classical Italian style; the type is italic, giving
a light, flowing quality to this first edition in Italian.

38 Bidpai. *Arabic version. Kalīlah wa-Dimnah. English.* THE MORALL
PHILOSOPHIE OF DONI: drawne out of the auncient writers. A worke
first compiled in the Indian tongue, and afterwardes reduced into
diuers other languages: and now lastly Englished out of Italian by
Thomas North. London, Imprinted by H. Denham [1570] 111 l.
19 cm.   PR2326.N6M7 1570 Rosenwald Coll

☆   In four parts, the third and fourth with special halftitles.
Sir Thomas North produced the earliest English version of the
fables of Bidpai, which he translated from Antonio Francesco Doni's
La Moral Filosophia del Doni, published in 1552. The full-page
woodcuts are clear and depict lively action.

39 Bidpai. *Arabic version. Kalīlah wa-Dimnah.* KITĀB KALĪLAH WA-
DIMNAH. United Arab Republic [1941] 51, 309 p. 30 cm.

PJ7741.B5 1941

☆   A modern edition in Arabic, with the text enclosed in ornamental
borders and with 13 mounted colored plates by Roman Strackalovsky
(the one of the monkey and the crocodile is upside down) in the style
of Persian miniatures. The introduction mentions the important
scholars and editions of this work.

40 Bidpai. NOTICE D'UN MANUSCRIT HÉBREU DE LA BIBLIOTHÈQUE
IMPERIALE, n.º 510, contenant un fragment de la version
hébraique du livre de Calila et Dimna, ou Fables de Bidpai, le roman
intitulé Paraboles de Sendabad, et divers autres traités. Par m. Silvestre de Sacy. *In* Notices et extraits des manuscrits de la Bibliothèque
nationale et autres bibliothèques. t. 9, 1. ptie. Paris, 1813. p. 397–
466.   Z6620.F8P2, v. 9, pt. 1

Detailed descriptions of this Hebrew manuscript comparing the
Hebrew with the Sanskrit include textual criticism and comments.

The translation is derived from the Latin of Giovanni da Capua and the subsequent Hebrew translation of the Rabbi Joel. The author, known as an important French orientalist, gives a short history of the Kalīlah and Dimnah versions of Giovanni da Capua, Firenzuola, Doni, and others.

41 Bidpai. *Arabic version. Kalīlah wa-Dimnah.* CALILA ET DIMNA, OU FABLES DE BIDPAI, en arabe; précédées d'un mémoire sur les diverses traductions qui en ont été faites dans l'Orient, et suivies de la Moallaka de Lébid, en arabe et en françois; par m. Silvestre de Sacy. Paris, Imprimerie royale, 1816.   140, 316 p. 26 cm.

PJ7741.B5   1816   Orien. Arab

☆   This famous version, the first European publication of the Arabic text, was edited from the version of Abdallah ibn al-Moqaffa by the great orientalist Silvestre de Sacy, who also made a French translation. In the "Memoire Historique" de Sacy gives an account of the many other languages into which it had been translated—Arabic, Greek, Hebrew, later Persian, and modern European languages.

42 Bidpai.   LIVRE DE CALILA ET DIMNA, translated en persan par Abou-'lmaali Nasr-allah fils de Mohammed fils d'Abd-Alhamid, de Gazna. Manuscrits persans de la Bibliothèque du roi, nos. 375, 376, 377, 379, 380, et 385.   Par m. Silvestre de Sacy.   *In* Notices et extraits des manuscrits de la Bibliothèque nationale et autres bibliothèques.   t. 10, 1. ptie.   Paris, 1818.   p. 94–196, 265–268, 427–432.

Z6620.F8P3, v. 10, pt. 1

Silvestre de Sacy traces the historical background of the Persian translation and of its versions and their relation to the Sha-nameh. He discusses the story of Burzuyeh and adds a chart comparing the order of chapters in the Persian, the Latin of Giovanni da Capua, and the Greek of Siméon Seth.

43 Bidpai. *Arabic version. Kalīlah wa-Dimnah. Syriac.* KALILAH AND DIMNAH; OR, THE FABLES OF BIDPAI: being an account of their literary history, with an English translation of the later Syriac version of the same, and notes, by I. G. N. Keith-Falconer. Cambridge, University Press, 1885.   LXXXV, 320 p.   PN989.I5B4   1885

The introduction gives a detailed analysis of the origins of the various parts or chapters, indicating which are Indian, Persian, or Arabic.   Synopses of the longer stories and chapters follow, and a careful, readable translation of the 21 parts.   In the notes and corrections Sanskrit, Syriac, and other such words are analyzed and compared.

44 Bidpai. *Arabic version. Kalīlah wa-Dimnah. English.* THE EARLIEST ENGLISH VERSION OF THE FABLES OF BIDPAI, "The morall

philosophie of Doni" by Sir Thomas North . . . edited and induced by Joseph Jacobs. London, D. Nutt, 1888. lxxx, 257 p. (Bibliothèque de Carabas. v. 3)　　　　　　　　　　PR2326.N6M7　1888

A reprint of the first edition of 1570, this contains reproductions of the early illustrations. The English scholar and folklorist has written a long introduction giving the history of Bidpai, with a chart of a "Pedigree of the Bidpai literature."

Joseph Jacobs' collection for children, *Indian Fairy Tales* (London, D. Nutt, 1892. 255 p.), contains seven fables with notes and sources.

45　Chauvin, Victor C. BIBLIOGRAPHIE DES OUVRAGES ARABES ou relatifs aux Arabes publiés dans l'Europe de 1810 à 1885. v. 2. Liège, H. Vaillant-Carmanne, 1897. 239 p.　　　　　　　　　　Z7052.C511

The compiler of this bibliography of *Kalilah wa-Dimnah* includes a thorough and complete listing of everything—books, articles, chapters, notices—in the European languages, with *éditions orientales* and manuscripts given in footnotes. Résumés of the tales, chapter by chapter, are followed by notations of the pages on which they appear in various translations and studies. The author lists the languages into which *Kalilah* has been translated, borrowings such as Reynard the Fox and La Fontaine, and the use of the fables in emblems and analogues, also giving résumés of the stories and notes. A table shows the relationship of the versions and translations (after p. vii).

ANVĀR-I SUHAILĪ

46　Bidpai. *Persian version. Anvār-i Suhailī. English. Harris. 1784.* THE INSTRUCTIVE AND ENTERTAINING FABLES OF PILPAY, an ancient Indian philosopher, containing a number of excellent rules for the conduct of persons of all ages, and in all stations; under several heads. 4th ed., corrected, improved, and enlarged. [Newport, R.I.] 1784. 119 p. 20 cm.　　　　　　　　　　PN989.I5B4　1784

☆　This rare first American edition (from the London edition) is not particularly attractive and has no illustrations. It is remodeled from J. Harris' translation of Gaulmin's French version, which was adapted from the Persian translation of Husain Va'iz.

47　Bidpai. *Persian version. Anvār-i Suhailī. English.* THE ANVÁR-I SUHAILÍ; OR, THE LIGHTS OF CANOPUS; being the Persian version of the fables of Pilpay; or the book "Kalílah and Damnah," rendered into Persian by Husain Vá'iz U'l Káshifí: literally translated, by E. B. Eastwick. Hertford, S. Austin, 1854. xxvii, 650 p. 25 cm.　　　　　　　　　　PN989.I5B4　1854　Rare Bk

The translator's preface gives an account of the early migrations and translations of the *Anvār-i Suhailī* and compares it, book by book, with the Panchatantra and Hitopadeśa. The first seven books, or two-thirds of the whole, were borrowed chiefly from these earlier Sanskrit writings, while books 8 through 12 contain in addition many Persian stories not related to the Sanskrit. Eastwick's translation keeps the prose and verse arrangement, with couplets, verses, and hemistichs being thus translated. Books 1 and 2 contain the story of Kalīlah and Dimnah; the later chapters return to the king and the Brahman.

48 ――― THE ANWÁR-I-SUHAILÍ; OR, LIGHTS OF CANOPUS, commonly known as Kalīlah and Damnah, adapted by Mullá Husaine ibn 'Alí al Wái'z-al-Káshifí from the fables of Bídpai; translated from the Persian by Arthur N. Wollaston. London, J. Murray, 1904. xviii, 504 p. 32 cm.   PN989.15B4   1904

☆   A large, attractive book with ornamental borders around each page, half of them printed in gold.   Earlier editions appeared in 1877 and 1894.

An important translation, complete and idiomatic, this gives the stories in the 14 books, with a long and elaborate introduction. Footnotes correct inaccuracies in the text and provide some necessary explanations.

"Elegance of style," Mr. Wollaston says in the introduction, "has throughout been sacrificed to closeness of translation. Doubtless certain pages would read more agreeably to English ears, curtailed of the many lengthy and entangled sentences, which are characteristic of the Oriental school of thought, but in view of the idea with which the work was undertaken none of these could be expunged."

49   Wilkinson, James V. S.   THE LIGHTS OF CANOPUS, ANVĀR I SUHAILĪ, described by J. V. S. Wilkinson. [London] The Studio [1929]   53 p. xxxvi mounted col. pl. 25.5 cm.   ND3399.B5W5

☆   Description of a 17th-century Mogul manuscript, Additional 18,579 in the British Museum, with reproduction of its miniatures.

Introductory chapter 4 gives the stories and their history. In 1570 Sir Thomas North published what corresponds to the earlier parts of *The Lights of Canopus,* entitled *The Morall Philosophie of Doni,* a lively specimen of Elizabethan writing and the first literary link between India and England.   From the French version, *Fables de Pilpay* or *Le Livre des Lumières,* which was familiar to La Fontaine, came the models for some of his fables.

The illustrations are dated in the year 1019 of the Hegira, which corresponds to A.D. 1610 or 1611. Wilkinson gives detailed descriptions of each of the 36 colored plates, which are mounted on heavy paper. *The Lights of Canopus* contains over a hundred stories, but the summaries and notes are confined to the 14 which the miniatures illustrate.

50 Frere, Mary E. I. OLD DECCAN DAYS; or, Hindoo fairy legends current in southern India. Collected from the oral tradition by M. Frere. With an introduction and notes by Sir Bartle Frere. Philadelphia, Lippincott, 1868. 345 p. PZ8.1.F8902

Some fables, two from Bidpai, are included in this book of stories collected from the author's ayah, Anna Liberata de Souza, "set down with scrupulous care, and supported by precise notes by Sir Bartle Frere." "The Narrator's Narrative" by Anna is a valuable record of the oral tradition in India.

These tales are charmingly told, not too elaborately but full of opulence, of gold, jewels, and beautiful princesses. Eloise Ramsey, in *Folklore for Children and Young People* (Philadelphia, American Folklore Society, 1952), said they were "among the landmarks in the literature of the folk tale."

51 Steel, Flora (Webster). TALES OF THE PUNJAB TOLD BY THE PEOPLE. With illustrations by J. Lockwood Kipling. London, New York, Macmillan, 1894. 395 p. PZ8.1.S813Tal

Five of these are fables; three are cumulative tales. R. C. Temple has provided notes, p. 299–326, analyses of the tales on the plan adopted by the Folklore Society of England, p. 327–355, and a survey of the incidents in modern Indian folktales, p. 356–395, dividing them into 4 classes with 35 major headings and many subheadings.

These lively versions provide an excellent text for children to read.

52 Bidpai. THE TORTOISE AND THE GEESE, and other fables of Bidpai, retold by Maude B. Dutton and illustrated by E. Boyd Smith. Boston, Houghton Mifflin, 1908. 124 p. PN989.I5B4

☆ A good selection from these ancient tales, well told in easy-to-read form and large print for young children. Their source is not indicated. Simple black-and-white line drawings by an artist who also illustrated a collection of Aesop's fables (New York, Century, 1911).

53 Bidpai. *Persian version. Anvār-i Suhailī.* A JACKAL IN PERSIA, by Major C. F. MacKenzie. Illustrated by KOS (Baroness Dombrowski). Garden City, N.Y., Doubleday, 1928. 210 p. PZ8.2.B47Ja

☆ A lively, vigorous retelling for children of the story of Kalīlah and Dimnah (Lilah and Damnah here) from the first three books of *Anvār-i Suhailī.* The main story is intact, and many of the subordinate tales are also included, but rearranged to form a logical whole. Some, at least, of the oriental feeling has been preserved in the style.

54 Mukerji, Dhan G. HINDU FABLES, FOR LITTLE CHILDREN. With many illustrations by Kurt Wiese. New York, E. P. Dutton [1929] 113 p. PZ8.2.M896Hi

☆   Told in a chatty, intimate style (the hare becomes "Bunny"), these 10 stories which the author remembered hearing from his nurse include 4 fables from the Panchatantra or related sources.

55   Ramaswami Raju, P. V., *ed.* INDIAN FABLES. With 18 plates by F. Carruthers Gould. London, Swan Sonnenschein, 1901. 129 p.

PN989.I5R3

Many unknown as well as familiar fables, over 100 altogether. No notes or sources are given.

56   Steel, Flora (Webster). THE TIGER, THE BRAHMAN, AND THE JACKAL. From *Tales of the Punjab* by Flora Annie Steel. With pictures by Mamoru Funai. New York, Holt, Rinehart and Winston, °1963. [25] p. 29 cm.

PZ8.1.S818Ti

☆   One of the most familiar of the Indian fables, told in Flora Steel's English manner. The amusing pictures have rich blues and greens as background for the golden tiger and crafty jackal, in this example of a single fable profusely illustrated for young children.

Aesop

Woodcut from Aesop's Vita et Fabulae (*Strassburg, Knoblochtzer, ca. 1481*). *Aesop surrounded by the symbols of many of his fables.* (*Item 60*)

AESOP

In his *Histories,* written in the fifth century B.C., Herodotus states that Aesop was a slave belonging to Iadmon, a citizen of Samos, and that he met a violent death about the middle of the sixth century at the hands of the people of Delphi.

The traditional biographies by later writers such as Maximus Planudes, a learned monk who died in 1310, can hardly be considered authentic. He makes Aesop a Phrygian slave who came to Athens in the sixth century B.C. By his telling of fables he secured his freedom, but he was put to death after he incurred the enmity of powerful persons whom he satirized. Classical scholars are not sure that such a person ever existed; but his name was attached to the fables by Greek writers from the fifth century on, and Aristophanes used it for comic effect. Some fables, however, appeared in Greek literature as early as Hesiod, two centuries before Aesop's presumed birth.

The first written collection in Greek, made about 300 B.C. by one Demetrius of Phalerum, has been lost but may have been the basis for later Greek manuscripts; a much later collection by Babrius, in verse, was also lost until the 19th century. The Greek fables were familiar in ancient Rome, however, and were known in the Middle Ages through their Latin form. The Latin verse collection of Phaedrus, a freedman of the first century, was preserved in a prose paraphrase by a writer of the 10th century who called himself Romulus. Many versions in Latin and other languages were derived from Romulus; they bear some form of the name Aesop, such as the Old French Ysopet, the Italian Esopo, or the Spanish Ysopo.

In the 12th century the prose of Romulus was put into Latin verse by a certain Walter of England (Gualterus Anglicus), whose text came to be known as the *Aesopus Moralisatus* of the Anonymus Neveleti, because it was printed at Frankfort in 1610 in the *Mythologia Aesopica* of Isaac Nevelet. This collection also included fables of Avianus, Abstemius of Urbino, and others. It had been printed before, however, and there were many editions from the 15th century on. The text of all the Latin fables from Phaedrus to the end of the medieval period was published in 5 volumes by Leopold Hervieux as *Les Fabulistes latins* (item 116).

The best known collection in Old French is that of Marie de France, written in England before 1200, based in part on a lost English translation from Romulus. The Old French *Ysopet-Avionnet* was a 14th-century Avianus.

"The Accursiana recension," the first collection to be published in Greek after the invention of printing, was named from the first edition (about 1479) by Bonus Accursius, who recast the fables on the basis of earlier recensions. Important modern scholarly editions of Aesop include those of

Karl Felix von Halm—*Fabulae Aesopicae Collectae, ex Recognitione Caroli Halmii* (Leipzig, Teubner, 1872. PA3851.A2)—and August Hausrath—*Corpus Fabularum Aesopicarum* (Leipzig, Teubner, 1940. PA3403.A325).

Perry, on p. 160 of the *Life and Fables of Aesop* (item 119), says: "Since there was probably never, at least in later times, any standard text of the fables, it was inevitable that both the range and their style of composition should change in accordance with the literary fashions of the day and the fancy of individual authors." For example, the classical fables did not state a moral in so many words; either the fable made its point or it did not. The moral comes from the *gātha* of the Jātakas. During the 18th and 19th centuries, however, this appendage to the fable, in English at least, often overpowered the short incident which illustrated it.

The first printed edition of Aesop in English was that produced by William Caxton in 1484 "at Westmynster in thabbey." Caxton himself made the translation from an earlier French version, and this seems to have been the standard English version for at least a century. Unfortunately, the Library of Congress does not own a copy.

The Reynard the Fox cycle has been mentioned in the note on Bidpai. It is a beast epic, an independent genre developed in the Middle Ages parodying the epics of chivalry. It contains episodes based on fables and in turn gave rise to new fables. The origin of these "fox poems" is found in certain medieval Latin works, such as the poem *Ysengrimus* written in 1148. Other types of literature allied to the fable are the fabliau, a short, realistic humorous story or conte; and the bestiary, in which descriptions of the traditional characteristics of animals are accompanied by symbolical or ethical interpretations. The medieval books of emblems also show symbolic pictures interpreted by fables, proverbs, or maxims.

It is true especially in this section that no real distinction can be made between editions for children and those for adults. Children deserve to see the fine artwork in adult books as well as in their own editions.

Incunabula

57 Aesopus. VITA ET FABULAE. German. [Augsburg, Anton Sorg, ca. 1479] [37], xxviii (*i.e.* cxxviii), [15] l., with errors in foliation. fol. 30 cm.   Incun. X.A28   Rosenwald Coll

☆   Compiled and translated by Heinrich Steinhöwel. The first edition of this translation was that of Johann Zainer at Ulm, about 1476–77.

Contains Vita, after the version of Rinuccio; Fabulae, after the prose version of Romulus; Fabulae extravagantes; Fabulae novae, after the version of Rinuccio; Fabulae, by Avianus; Fabulae collectae, by Petrus Alfonsi, Poggio, and others; and De duobus amantibus, by Leonardo Aretino Bruni (translated by Niclas von Wyle).

The Gothic text is clear and perfectly balances the simple lines of the woodcuts. These show much action, often combining two incidents from a fable in the same picture. The frontispiece, the

Woodcut from Aesop's Vita et Fabulae *(Augsburg, Anton Sorg, ca. 1479).*
The Fox and the Crane. (Item 57)

familiar woodcut of Aesop, pictures him as a hunchback surrounded
by characters from his fables.

Three other copies are known: one in Dresden, one in the Victoria
and Albert Museum in London, and one in the Metropolitan Museum
in New York.

58 ———— VITA ET FABULAE LATINE. [Augsburg, Anton Sorg, ca. 1480]
130 l. fol. 26 cm.   Incun. X.A29   Rare Bk

The frontispiece, showing Aesop surrounded by the animals, and
the other 191 woodcuts are printed from the same blocks as the edition
printed by Zainer in Ulm about 1476–77. Some fables begin with
woodcut initials and some have initial spaces not filled in.

The fables consist of the Latin version (without the German) which
was used in the original edition of Steinhöwel's *Aesop*.

59 ———— AESOPIA VITA PER MAXIMUM PLANUDEM et ejusden fabulae
gr. cum versione lat. Rinutii. Thessali [Mediolani] Bonus Accursius
[ca. 1480] [70] l. 4°. 22.5 cm. Lacks pts. 2–3 (l. 71–168).
                                                    Incun. X.A25   Rare Bk

☆   This Milan edition of Bonus Accursius is known as the Accursiana
recension. Part 1 is the first edition of the Greek text, of which this
is the largest and finest copy known.

que ad me de te recurrit·Lupus non erubuit veritate·ac ma
ledicis mihi inquit·Agnus ait·non maledixi tibi·at lup9 et
ante sex menses ita pater tuus mihi fecit Agnus ait·nec ego
tunc natus eram·At lupus denuo ait·agrū mihi pascendo
deuastasti·Agnus inquit·cum dentibus careaz·quomodo id
facere potui·lupus dentium ira concitus ait liez tua nequeā
soluere argumenta·cenare tamen opipare intendo ·agnum
qz cepit·innocentiiqz vitam eripuit ac māducauit·¶ Fabu
la significat ꝙ apud improbos calumniatores·ratio et ve
ritas non habent locum·

¶ Fabula Tercia de rana et mure·

Vris iter rumpente lacu venit obuiam muri
m   Rana loquax·et opem pacta nocere cupit
      Omne genus pestis·superat mens dissona verbis
Cum sentes animi florida lingua polit·
Rana sibi murem filo confederat·audet·
Nectere fune pedem·rumpere fraude fidem·
Pes cogit ergo pedem·sed mens a mente recedit
Ambo natant·trahitur ille·sed illa trahit·
Mergitur·vt secum murem demergat·amico
Naufragium faciens·naufragat ipsa fidem·

                           d   iiij·

Page from Aesop's Vita et Fabulae Latine *(Augsburg, Anton Sorg, ca. 1480).*
The Frog and the Mouse. *(Item 58)*

60 ——— Vɪᴛᴀ ᴇᴛ ꜰᴀʙᴜʟᴀᴇ. Latin. [Strassburg, Heinrich Knoblochtzer, ca. 1481] [114] l.   Incun. X.A285 Rosenwald Coll

☆ Compiled by Heinrich Steinhöwel and originally published ca. 1477
at Ulm by Johann Zainer.

Contains Vita, translated by Rinuccio; Fabulae, books 1–4 in the
prose version of Romulus and metrical version of books 1–3 of the
Anonymus Neveleti; Fabulae extravagantes; Fabulae novae, translated by Rinuccio; Fabulae, by Avianus; Fabulae collectae, by Petrus
Alfonsi, Poggio, and others.

Initials, initial strokes, and paragraph marks are supplied in red.
This copy has the original leather binding, stamped brass corners,
center piece, and clasps.

The edition is similar to the Augsburg of 1479, containing clear
strong woodcuts, with angular figures, very much like the ones in that
edition and obviously copied from them, but rougher, cruder, and
with less detail. Elaborate initials (not colored) are in a different,
more sophisticated style. Two alternating borders are decorated with
insects, animals, and intertwining plants.

Woodcuts from Aesop's Vita et Fabulae *(Strassburg, Knoblochtzer, ca. 1481)*
The Lion and the Fox, The Ass and the Wolf. (Item 60)

61 ———— FABULAE. Brescia, Jacobus de Britannicus, 2 Dec. 1485. 4°. 21.8 cm. Vollbehr Coll

☆ An edition of *Aesopus Moralisatus,* the metrical version of the Anonymus Neveleti, without illustrations. Spaces are left for initials but only the first is filled in. A vellum page from a choir book has been used for the cover.

62 ———— VITA ET AESOPUS MORALISATUS. Latin and Italian. Naples [Germani fidelissimi for] Francesco del Tuppo, 13 Feb. 1485. [168] l. ; [1] [44] and [168] (all blanks) lacking. fol. 27.5 cm.
Incun. 1485.A35 Rosenwald Coll

☆ Aesop's Life in the Latin translation of Rinuccio; the Fables in the Latin metrical version of the Anonymus Neveleti, known as *Aesopus Moralisatus.* The Italian translation and additions are by Francesco del Tuppo. The text is set in clear Roman type.
The woodcuts are particularly lively, with humorous expressions on the animals' faces. The decorative borders, often repeated, have a Spanish flavor and are very handsome, with grotesques in the curved upper portion. In the illustrations for his Life, Aesop is not deformed but has short hair and heavy features.

63 ———— VITA ET FABULAE. Latin. Antwerp, Gerardus Leeu, Sept. 26, 1486. 104 l. fol. 26.8 cm.
Incun. 1486.A3 Rosenwald Coll

☆ The "Fabulae et vita Esopi" translated by Rinuccio and fables of Avianus, Petrus Alphonsi, and Poggio as compiled by Steinhöwel and originally published ca. 1477 at Ulm by Zainer.
The illustrations are charming, many of them showing scenes of farm life with 15th-century houses and fences; the frontispiece is the familiar one of Aesop with a border of his characters. Initials and paragraph marks in red or blue; initial strokes in red.

64 ———— FABULAE ITALICE ET LAT. PER ACCIUM ZUCCUM. Brescia, Boninus de Boninis Ragusimus, 7 Mar. 1487. 4°.
Hain 348 Vollbehr Coll

☆ The *Aesopus Moralisatus* with interlinear additions of Accio Zucco in Italian. The first eight leaves of the Library of Congress copy are facsimiles.
The drawing of the woodcuts is angular, in light lines; some shading and details such as windows have been added later. Spaces are left for initials.

65 ———— [Another edition, ca. 1487] Incun. 1487.A3 Rare Bk
The only known copy, and it in fragmentary form, the first 10 leaves and some others missing. The cuts are the same as in the edition above, but the text is slightly different.

Woodcut from Vita et Aesopus Moralisatus (*Naples, Francesco del Tuppo, 1485*).
The Hares and the Frogs. (*Item 62*)

Woodcut from Aesopus Moralisatus (*Venice, Manfredus de Bonellis, 1493*).
The Frog and the Fox. (*Item 71*)

36

66 ——— AESOPUS MORALISATUS CUM BONO CŌMENTO. [Cologne. Heinrich Quantell, 1489] 41 l. 4°.   Hain 304 Vollbehr Coll

67 ——— [Another edition] 1491.   Hain 309 Vollbehr Coll
An *Aesop* printed in fine Gothic type, in Latin with interlinear comment in smaller type, also in Latin. It contains no illustrations except for exquisite red or blue initials.

68 ——— FABULAE. French. [Paris, Antoine Vérard, ca. 1490] [36] l.; leaves [23]–[36] lacking. fol. 28.5 cm.
Incun, 1490.A2 Rosenwald Coll

☆   The first leaf contains the title *Les apologues et fables de Laurens Valle trāslatees de latin en francois.* The translation from the Latin version of Lorenzo Valla is by Guillaume Tardiff.
Small, crude, but lively woodcuts are repeated over and over again throughout the book. Green and yellow color has been added here and there, carelessly (by a child?). Initials are supplied in red; titles and the Moral are underlined in red.

69 ——— AESOPUS MORALISATUS. Latin and Italian. Venice, Manfredus de Bonellis, de Monteferrato, 1491. [72] l. 4°.
Hain 349 Vollbehr Coll

☆   One of the four extant copies of the first edition of what is, according to Burger, the first book printed by Manfredus de Bonellis at Venice. It is in Latin blackletter with Accio Zucco's additions in Italian verse.
The 66 illustrations are, as Bonellis modestly states, "wonderful and celebrated woodcuts"; each is enclosed in an elaborate decorative border usually filling one-half to three-fourths of the page. This is the first edition with these woodcuts, which are smaller copies of those used in earlier editions. Most of them have been colored in fine detail, even with trees and backgrounds added to the originals by hand.

70 ——— VITA ET FABULAE E GRAECO LATINA par Rinucium, cum Extravagantibus, fabulis Aviani, Alphonsi Collectis ex Poggio, etc. [Basel, Michael Furter, ca. 1492]   Hain 327 Vollbehr Coll
An edition illustrated with 193 woodcuts based on the familiar ones of the Sorg edition of 1479 (item 57). The frontispiece shows Aesop as a hunchback, surrounded by the symbols of his fables.

71 ——— AESOPUS MORALISATUS. Latin and Italian. Venice, Manfredus de Bonellis, de Monteferrato, 17 Aug. 1493. [72] l. 4°. 19 cm.
Incun. 1493.A3 Rosenwald Coll
The Latin metrical version of the Anonymus Neveleti, known as

37

Aesopus Moralisatus, with Italian translation (also in verse) and additions by Accio Zucco. A full-page woodcut on the first leaf (title page) has the inscription *Esopus.*

The charming and humorous woodcuts suffer from being printed in light ink on thin paper.

72 ──── Fabulae. [Naples, Cristannus Preller, ca. 1495] [10] l. 8°. 21.5 cm. Incun. X.A26 Rosenwald Coll

A small collection in Lorenzo Valla's translation. The only illustration, a frontispiece, is a full-page woodcut of Aesop.

73 ──── Fabulae selectae graece et latine ex interpretatione Rinutii, editae a Bono Accursio. Reggio d'Emilia, Dionysius Berthochus, 1497. Mo. 674 Thacher Coll

A later edition of the Accursiana recension containing 62 fables with the Greek and Latin text printed in two parallel columns on each page. The dedication reads: "Bonus Accursius Pisanus doctissimo ae sapientissimo ducali Quaestori Johanni francisco Turriano salutem plurimam decit."

74 ──── Vita et aesopus moralisatus. Latin and Italian. Milan, Guillermi Le Signerre fratres for Gotardus da Ponte, 15 Sept. 1498. [38] l. 4°. 20.2 cm. Incun. 1498.A35 Rosenwald Coll

☆ The title on leaf 1 reads: *Esopo con la uita sua historiale et uulgare.* The text, in Gothic type, repeats that of the 1493 Naples edition. It includes Aesop's life in the Latin of Rinuccio, translated into Italian by Francesco del Tuppo.

The woodcuts—23 in the text, plus a border to the title page and initials—were made by a Milanese artist and are characteristic of Lombard art. They are small, bold, and nicely proportioned to their space.

Editions of the 16th to 18th Centuries

75 Aesopus. Esopi appologi siue mythologi cum quibusdam carminum et fabularum additionibus Sebastiani Brant. [Basilee, Impressi opera et impensa Jacobi de Phortzheim, 1501] 408 p. 30 cm. PA8230.A1 1501 Rosenwald Coll

☆ In two parts: the first includes Aesop's life in the Latin of Rinuccio, the fables in the prose version of Romulus and the metrical version of the Anonymus Neveleti, and the fables of Avianus, Rinuccio, and others, with additions and commentary by Brant; the second part contains a collection of fables adapted from various authors by Sebastian Brant, who also wrote the medieval satire *Ship of Fools.*

Woodcuts in the first part of this large Aesop are similar to those of the Sorg edition of 1479, including the familiar portrait of Aesop

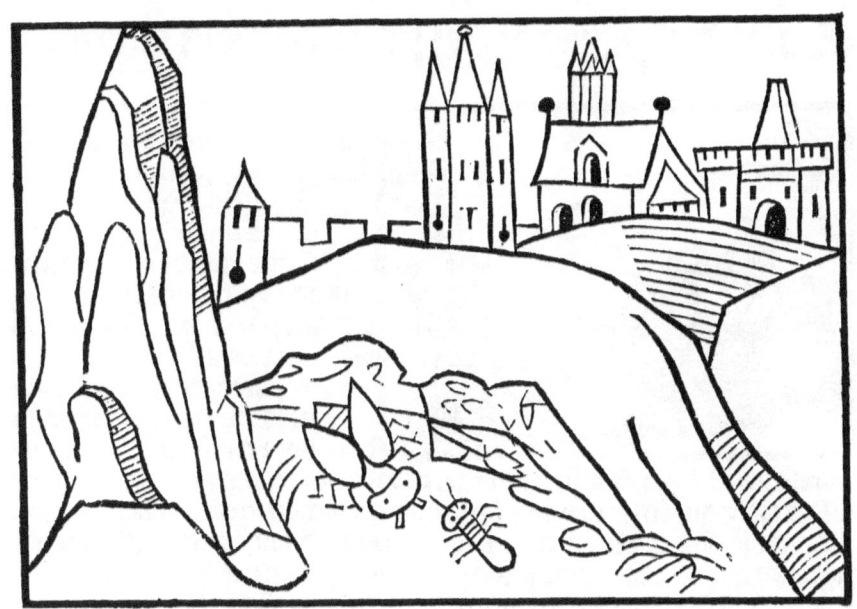

Woodcut from Esopi Appologi Siue Mythologi (*Basel, Jacobi de Phortzheim, 1501*).
The Grasshopper and the Ant. (*Item 75*)

as a frontispiece; the illustrations in the second part are less primitive.
Many, including the frontispiece, have been hand colored.

76 ──── LIBRO DEL SABIO Y CLARISSIMO FABULADOR YSOPO hystoriado y
annotado. [Seville, J. Cronberger, 1521] lxxx l. 31 cm.
PA3855.S7R5   Rosenwald Coll

☆   A Spanish edition containing La vida de Ysopo; Las fabulas de
Ysopo (books 1–4); Las fabulas extrauagantes; Fabulas del Ysopo de
la trasladacion nueua de Remicio; Las fabulas de Auiano; Las fabulas
collectas de Alfonso, de Pogio, y de otros.
This prose translation is beautifully printed, with clear, wide
margins. The one or two small woodcuts on each page are charming,
but poorly proportioned and awkwardly drawn. The morals are
printed on scrolls in the margins with a hand pointing to each one.
Decorated initials.

77 ──── AESOPI FABVLAE CVM VVLGARI INTERPRETATIONE: & figuris
acri cura emendatae. Brixiae, Apud Loduicum Britannicum, 1537.
[64] p. 21 cm.   PA8230.A1   1537   Rosenwald Coll

☆   The Latin metrical version of the Anonymus Neveleti, known as
Aesopus Moralisatus, with Latin commentary and Italian interlinear
translation.

39

La.v.del perro y del pedaço dela carne.

Las vezes pier∕ de el cobdicioso lo que tiene en su po∕ der queriendo to∕ mar lo ageno:delo qual se dize tal fabula. El perro teniendo vn pedaço de carne: lo passaua por vn rio: enl qual vio la sombra dela carne que el lle∕ uaua: τ pareciédo le aquella ma yor que la que el tenia: abrio la boca para tomar la sombra que parescia enel agua. E assi se le cayo el pedaço dela carne dela boca: τ lleuo se lo el rio:y quedo sin lo vno τ sin lo otro perdiendo lo que tenia:pensando alcançar lo otro que le parescia mayor:lo qual no pudo auer. Esta fabula significa que no deue hombre codiciando lo ageno τ dubdoso dexar lo suyo que es cierto:avn que lo q codicia le parezca mas. E assi segú el prouerbio comun:quien todo lo quiere todo lo pierde.

From Libro del sabio y clarissimo fabulador Ysopo (*Seville, Cronberger, 1521*).
The Dog and the Shadow of the Meat. (*Item 76*)

The woodcuts are small, spaced one or two to a page, and show a relationship to earlier woodcuts, such as those in the Sorg edition of 1479. The figures are placed in the same way, but the drawing has less humor.

78 ——— AESOPI PHRYGIS FABVLAE GRAECE ET LATINÈ, cum alijs opus-culis, quorum index proxima refertur pagella. Basileae, per Ioannem Heruagium, 1544. 364, [3] p. PA3851.A2 1544

☆ Bound in stamped leather over wooden boards; the prophets "Daniel, Esaias, Ezechiel, and Ieremias" appear in four panels sur-rounding a central panel, with conventional fleur-de-lis ornaments.
This reprint of the Basel edition of J. Froben, 1518, includes the Planudes version of the Life as well as the Fables. The Greek text is printed on the versos, the Latin translation, in part by A. P. Manuzio, on the opposite rectos. There are no illustrations.

79 [Deene, Edward de] DE WARACHTIGHE FABULEN DER DIEREN. Bruges, Pieter de Clerck, 26 Aug. 1567. 216, [6] p. 20 cm.
PT5645.D4W3 1567 Rosenwald Coll

☆ This rare volume contains the fables of Aesop in a Flemish adapta-tion in verse by Edward de Deene. The 108 copperplate illustrations of great detail are the work of Marcus Gheeraerts. Wenceslaus Hollar based his later illustrations for Ogilby's English translation (item 82) on them.

80 Bullokar, William. AESOPZ FABLZ IN TRU ORTOGRAPHY with Grammar-notz. Her-untoo ar also jooined the short sentencez of the wyz Cato. Translated out-of Latin in-too English. *In* Plessow, Max. Geschichte der fabeldichtung in England bis zu John Gay (1726). Nebst neudreck von Bullokars "Fables of Aesop" 1585. Berlin, Mayer & Müller, 1906. p. 3–235.   PD25.P3, no. 52

This 16th-century curiosity was compiled by an early spelling reformer and first published by Edmund Bollifant (London, 1585). Bullokar was also a moralist, for his Life of Aesop dwells on the fabulist's excellence "when he toucheth mortal discipline or way of life."

F. J. Harvey Darton, in his *Children's Books in England* (Cambridge, University Press, 1958, p. 11–12), said of Bullokar: "As a translator he is a little more ornate than Caxton. But in simplicity, in truth of aim, his English is almost startlingly removed from the contemporary literary style. . . . It is plain English, once more. Bullokar veritably wrote with a human young reader in his mind. Maybe he was, in our cant phrase, a crank. But he had a crank's honourable earnestness, downrightly expressed."

81 Aesopus. THE PHRYGIAN FABULIST; or, the Fables of Aesop: extracted from the Latine Copie, and moralized. By Leonard Willan Gent. London, Printed by W. D. for Nicolas Bourn, at the South Entrance of the Roial-Exchange, 1650. 15 l., 184 p. front. (port.) 16½ cm.   35/Fables/1650   Rare Bk

☆ An edition in rude verse which is the earliest English edition in the Library of Congress. It includes a Life of Aesop (22 p.) based on the Latin of Maximus Planudes. The political and social morals are given in verse. The printing is poor and uneven.

82 ―――― THE FABLES OF AESOP, PARAPHRAS'D IN VERSE; adorn'd with sculpture, and illustrated with annotations. 2d ed. by John Ogilby, esq. Master of His Majesties Revells in the Kingdom of Ireland. London, Printed by Thomas Roycroft for the author, 1668. 2 v. (211, 231 p.) 38 cm.   Fabyan Coll. 3   Rare Bk

☆ Ogilby's 1651 edition in English verse—the first "polite" edition meant for children as well as grownups—set a fashion in England before La Fontaine appeared in France. A different edition appeared in 1665 and was reissued in 1668, with engravings by Wenceslaus Hollar, an itinerant artist who came to England in the mid-17th century. His elegant engravings in semiclassical style combine a detailed observation of nature with landscapes of recognizable places. A few of them are borrowed from Gheeraerts (item 79). These productions are what a tradesman in books today would call a fine-art edition, with large plates of excellent quality.

Francis Barlow, who did the engravings for another edition of Ogilby's verse, later created a version of his own and in 1687, perhaps seeing La Fontaine's popularity, added a French text to the English verses of Mrs. Aphra Behn (item 85).

83   [Benserade, Isaac de]   FABLES D'ESOPE EN QUATRAINS dont il y en a une partie au Labyrinte de Versailles.   A Paris, Chez Sebastien Mabre-Cramoisy, 1678.   222 p.   16 cm.   PQ1715.A64

Benserade compressed some of Aesop's fables into French quatrains, which were graven on the pedestals of the figures representing the subjects of each fable that once stood in what was called the Labyrinth of Versailles.   Each fable in his book is illustrated with a small oval wood engraving.

84   LABYRINTE DE VERSAILLES.   A Paris, De l'Imprimerie royale, 1679. 34, 79 p.   22 cm.   NA9415.V4L25

☆   Delicate, detailed engravings by Sébastien Le Clerc of the fountains in the labyrinth in the gardens of Versailles, which represented 39 of Aesop's fables.   Prose epitomes of the fables and descriptive text are by Charles Perrault; metrical versions, one opposite each full-page engraving, are by Benserade.   A "Plan du Labyrinte" indicates the location of each fountain in the maze.   The first engraving shows the gateway, with high hedges on either side.   Unfortunately, the fountains were later destroyed, except for a few pieces of sculpture.

The first French edition appeared in 1677.   An English edition was published the following year as "Aesop in Court; or, the Labyrinth of Versailles," in *Ethic Amusements*, edited by Daniel Bellamy, Jr. (London, 1768.   PR3318.B14E7), delineated in French and English, with plates engraved by G. Bickham.   The translation was made by Daniel Bellamy, Sr.

85   AESOPUS.   AESOP'S FABLES, WITH HIS LIFE: in English, French and Latin.   Newly translated.   Illustrated with one hundred and twelve sculptures.   To this edition are likewise added, thirty one new figures representing his life.   By Francis Barlow.   London, Printed by H. Hills jun. for Francis Barlow, and are to be sold by Chr. Wilkinson, 1687.   40, 40, 17, 221 p.   32 x 20 cm.   PA3855.E55   1687

☆   The 40-page Life of Aesop, in English, is illustrated with 31 plates. The 110 fables in English verse by Mrs. Aphra Behn are printed on the plates below Barlow's engravings, the French and Latin on the opposite page.

The first edition (most copies of which were destroyed in the London fire) had the title *Aesop's Fables With His Life: In English, French & Latin; the English by Tho. Philipott Esq.; the French and Latin by Rob. Codrington, M.A., illustrated with one hundred and twelve sculptures by Francis Barlow* (London, Printed by William Godbid for Francis Barlow, 1666).

"Barlow's illustrations, published first in 1666, are freely, almost carelessly etched and have a pleasant, unsophisticated naturalism," says John McKendry in the Metropolitan Museum's *Aesop* (item 2).

86 L'Estrange, *Sir* Roger, *ed. and tr.* FABLES OF AESOP, AND OTHER EMINENT MYTHOLOGISTS: with morals and reflexions. London, R. Sare, 1692. 480 p.   PN981.L4 1692

☆   Bound with this work is a second part (238 p.), entitled *Fables and Storyes Moralized*, which was also published in London by R. Sare in 1699.

The edition is suited to the general reader, especially the young reader. L'Estrange collected and retranslated all available fables and rewrote the "morals" (the existing versions were so "insipid and flat" as to be "rather dangerous than profitable") and added his own "Reflexions."

Said to be the largest collection of fables in the English language, it contains 500 drawn not only from older writers like Phaedrus, Avianus, and others, but, in the second part, also from La Fontaine.

"The narrative is wordy compared with Caxton's or Bullokar's," F. J. Harvey Darton says in his *Children's Books in England* (p. 17), "but it has the right touch of truth and humour, and puts the fable in its proper period—the eternal day of 'Once upon a time.' One feels, too, that the man who made the translation enjoyed it himself."

87 Dodsley, Robert. SELECT FABLES OF ESOP, and other fabulists, in three books. Birmingham, Printed by John Baskerville for R. & J. Dodsley, 1761. 204, [28] p.   PN981.D6

☆   The first edition of Dodsley's fables, with Baskerville's fine type and many small, neat engravings. Each full page of illustrations contains 12 small, round medallion pictures, numbered to correspond to the fables. The Life of Aesop "collected from Ancient writers by Mons. De Meziriac" is translated into English with notes; a preliminary "Essay on Fable" is signed by Dodsley. Books 1 and 2 include Fables "from the Ancients" and "from the Moderns"; and Book 3 is "Fables Newly Invented" by Dodsley and his friends. Dodsley was a bookseller and publisher and a personal friend of Samuel Johnson, who called him "Doddy."

About Dodsley's translation F. J. Harvey Darton says in his *Children's Books in England* (p. 22): "The beasts, in *his* Fables, must always use language suitable to their acknowledged character. The Lion must speak in a kingly manner, the Owl with 'a pomp of phrase' which 'the buffoon monkey should avoid.' It is a most valuable asset in fiction that animals should have stock human characters; and, L'Estrange, Croxall, and Dodsley standardized those characters for juvenile consumption."

88 Aesopus. THE FABLES, with a life of the author, and embellished

with 112 plates. London, J. Stockdale, 1793. 2 v. ([189], 248 p.)
29 cm. PA3855.E5C7 1793 Rosenwald Coll

☆ An elaborately produced edition containing 110 fables in the translation of Samuel Croxall, with long moral applications, and a 57-page Life of Aesop. The fine, although dull, engravings are by various artists. Bound in the original lavender boards.

89 —— ÉSOPE, GREC ET LATIN, traduit en français par J.-B. Gail. A Paris, De l'imprimerie de Delance, l'an v. 1796. xx, 371 p. (Les trois fabulistes. [t. 1]) PN984.G3, t. 1

This edition is adapted from the 1550 collection of Basel, the Latin translation being that of Aldo Pio Manusio. The Greek and French are on opposite pages, with the Latin below, on both pages. The translator has written a preliminary discourse summarizing the theories about the life and person of Aesop.

90 —— AESOP'S FABLES; embellished with one hundred & eleven elegant engravings. London, T. Heptinstall [Printed by C. Whittingham, 1797] 267 p. 35/Fables Rare Bk

☆ Samuel Croxall's translation was first published by T. Tonson and J. Watts (London, 1722). Croxall, a prominent theologian of his day, intended his translation to supersede all others, especially that of Roger L'Estrange, 1692. And it nearly did, for most of his century. Following the preface is "A Catalogue of the various editions of Aesop's fables, in the original language, as well as in translation, from 1476 to 1796."
The 110 fables with their moral applications, are presented in an innocuous prose for children. They are of unequal merit and at times are lengthy but have a quaint humor. The small, pleasing illustrations are signed by various engravers.

91 —— FABULAE AESOPI SELECTAE; or, select fables of Aesop; with an English translation, more literal than any yet extant, designed for the readier instruction of beginners in the Latin tongue. By H. Clarke. Exeter, N. H., Printed by H. Ranlet, for Thomas and Andrews, E. Larkin and J. West, Boston, 1799. 132 p.
PA3855.A2 1799 Rare Bk

H. Clarke, a Latin teacher, edited a textbook of simplified fables in Latin in one column with the English translation in the opposite column. This is the "First Exeter edition, printed from the London 10th edition."

92 —— THE FABLES OF AESOP, AND OTHERS. With designs on wood, by Thomas Bewick. Newcastle, Printed by E. Walter, for T. Bewick, 1818. xxiv, 376 p. PA3855.E5B38 1818 Rosenwald Coll

☆ Dedicated "To the Youth of the British Isles." Bewick's introduc-

Wood engraving by Thomas Bewick from The Fables of Aesop *(Newcastle, E. Walter for T. Bewick, 1818). The Vain Jackdaw. (Item 92)*

tion gives a short history of the fable from "Veeshnu Sarma," Pilpay, Aesop, and Phaedrus to the English edition of Caxton in 1484. The homely moral applications attached to the fables may have contributed to the great popularity of Bewick's version.

Bewick popularized the technique of wood engraving, which consists of engraving the end grain of a block of hard wood with tools like those used to engrave metal and printing the cut, like a woodcut, at the same time as the type. He used the technique late in the 18th century when he did his first *Aesop* (Newcastle, 1784). "The revised editions of 1818 and 1823 are not among Bewick's best works and are on the whole surprisingly derivative considering his talent for animal illustration," John McKendry said in the Metropolitan Museum study *Aesop*. "He drew much from Croxall's metal cuts of 1722, which in turn were based mainly on the first illustrated La Fontaine of 1668 by Chauveau, which was itself to a great extent dependent on Barlow's and even Geeraert's earlier illustrations."

Later Editions

93 Aesopus. AESOP'S FABLES; a new version, chiefly from original sources, by Thomas James. With more than 50 illustrations designed by John Tenniel. New York, R. B. Collins [1848] 224 p. 22 cm.
PA3855.E5J3 1848

☆   A pleasant prose translation of 203 fables, which became the basis for many later versions.

"The translator's introduction is dated from Theddingworth Vicarage, January 1848. Though this was not the first book illustrated by John Tenniel, it brought about his introduction to *Punch.*" These neat engravings only suggest the satire of his later work.

94   ——— THE FABLES OF AESOP AND OTHERS translated into human nature. Designed and drawn on the wood by Charles H. Bennett. Engraved by Swain. London, W. Kent [1857]   21 l.   26.5 cm.

PN982.B4

☆   Each fable is printed opposite a large illustration, probably hand colored. Bennett's animals are caricatures with enlarged heads, clothed and acting like people.

95   ——— AESOP'S FABLES.   Illustrated by Ernest Griset.   With text based chiefly upon Croxall, La Fontaine, and L'Estrange.   Revised and re-written by J. B. Rundell.   London, New York, Cassell, Petter, and Galpin [1869]   244 p.   PZ8.2.A254Ru

The full-page wood engravings with dark backgrounds are reminiscent of Doré although at times more humorous.   Rundell has based his terse retellings on the two best earlier translations.

Walter Crane, in his autobiography, said of Ernest Griset: "His first important work was the illustration of an edition of *Aesop's Fables,* published by Messrs. Cassell."

96   ——— SOME OF AESOP'S FABLES with modern instances shewn in designs by Randolph Caldecott, from new translations by Alfred Caldecott, the engravings by J. D. Cooper.   New York, Macmillan, 1883.   79 p.   29 cm.   NC1115.C315   1883

☆   Following the suggestion of his engraver, Randolph Caldecott appended to each fable a humorous, modern scene, with social or political implications, instead of the traditional moral ending.   The translator, who was the artist's younger brother, was Dean of King's College, London, and Prebendary of St. Paul's Cathedral.   "The Translations aim at replacing the florid style of our older English versions, and the stilted harshness of more modern ones, by a plainness and terseness more nearly like the character of the originals."

97   Crane, Walter.   THE BABY'S OWN AESOP; being the fables condensed in rhyme, with portable morals pictorially pointed by Walter Crane.   Engraved & printed in colours by Edmund Evans.   London & New York, G. Routledge, 1887.   56 p.   18.5 x 19.5 cm.   PZ8.2.A254Cr

☆   Crane's are among the earliest Aesop illustrations using the new technique of photoetching, which simplified the reproduction of drawings.   They are Art Nouveau style in their use of pattern, line, and color.

Illustration by Walter Crane from his The Baby's Own Aesop (*London & New York, Routledge, 1887*). *The Fox and the Crane.* *(Item 97)*

In his preface Crane thanks his early master, W. J. Linton, for the use of his manuscript "The Wisdom of Aesop," in which he has condensed each fable into a limerick. Covers and end papers were designed by the artist.

98 Aesopus. AESOP'S FABLES; a new translation by V. S. Vernon Jones, with an introduction by G. K. Chesterton and illustrations by Arthur Rackham. New York, Garden City Publishing Co. [c1939] xxix, 224 p. 22.5 cm.   PZ8.2.A254Rac

☆   First published by William Heinemann of London in 1912, Jones' prose translation of 284 fables is illustrated with many black-and-white drawings (some full-page) and 13 color plates—Rackham's distinctive gnarled trees, well-dressed animals, and grotesque humans, in muted color and flowing line.

47

The introduction offers an unusual viewpoint and an enlightening appreciation.

99 ———— FABLES OF AESOP according to Sir Roger L'Estrange; with fifty drawings by Alexander Calder. Paris, Harrison; New York, Minton, Balch [1931] 124 p. 26 cm. PZ3855.E5L4 1931

☆ Dramatic, simple line drawings have been reproduced by photo-etching to illustrate this handsome edition of 201 fables.

100 ———— AESOP'S FABLES, edited and illustrated with wood engravings by Boris Artzybasheff. New York, Viking Press, 1933. 86 p. 24 cm. PZ8.2.A254Ar

☆ The text of these 90 fables combines the humor of the Croxall edition of 1722 and the imaginative detail of the James edition of 1848, to make "a livelier and gayer interpretation." The open format of the book and the handsome wood engravings—stylized designs—make an elegant production. The illustrated lining papers were also provided by the artist.

101 ———— AESOP'S FABLES; retold, illustrated with woodcuts and printed by Elfriede Abbe. Ithaca, N.Y., 1950. 70 p. 33 cm.
PA3855.E5A3

☆ Bold woodcuts are printed directly from the original blocks, and the text from hand-set type heavily inked to balance the strong pictures. The volume includes 122 fables—in brief versions, without special distinction.

102 ——— 12 FABLES OF AESOP. [Limited ed. New York, Museum of
Modern Art, 1964, c1954] [33] p. 28 cm. PZ8.2.A254Wf8

☆ "Linoleum blocks by Antonio Frasconi to illustrate Twelve Fables
of Aesop newly narrated by Glenway Wescott."

An elegant edition with striking, very black, modern prints that
resemble the 15th-century Aesops in their simplicity and vitality.
Titles are printed in red, for well-known fables retold in witty, im-
peccable prose: "The Starved Farmer and His Fat Dogs"; "The
Caged Nightingale and the Intelligent Bat"; "The Hare with Ability
and the Tortoise with Staying Power"; "The Jackdaw with Eclectic
Plumage"; and "The Flattered Raven and the Crafty Fox."

Several large original prints for the *Fables* are displayed in the
exhibit.

Frasconi has also published a collection of nine *Known Fables,*
illustrated in the same bold style (South Norwalk, Conn., 1964
PZ8.2.A254Fp). Only 500 were printed, at the Spiral Press in New
York, on folded leaves of Goyu paper from the original blocks. The
text, printed in red, is from the Newcastle edition of 1820 which was
illustrated with Thomas Bewick wood engravings.

Linoleum block by Antonio Frasconi for 12 Fables of Aesop. *Copyright © 1954 by
the Museum of Modern Art; reproduced by permission. The Fishermen With the
Stone in Their Net. (Item 102)*

Modern Editions for Children

103 Aesopus. THE FABLES OF AESOP; selected, told anew, and their history traced by Joseph Jacobs. Done into pictures by Richard Heighway. London and New York, Macmillan, 1894. 222 p.

PZ8.2.A254J

This collection of 82 fables still serves as a basic source in children's literature. A "Short History of the Aesopic Fable" summarizes all the essential conclusions reached in the first volume of Jacobs' definitive edition of *The Fables of Aesop As First Printed by William Caxton* (item 115). The selection comes from Caxton's *Aesop* with some additions from Babrius and Phaedrus retold "in such a way as would interest children." The "Pedigree of Aesop" and Jacobs' "Notes" at the end are valuable although they need revision by a folklorist to take into account more recent research.

104 Wiggin, Kate Douglas (Smith), *and* Nora Archibald Smith, *eds.* THE TALKING BEASTS; a book of fable wisdom. Illustrations by Harold Nelson. Garden City, N.Y., Doubleday, Page, 1911. 391 p.

PZ8.2.W639T

A general, useful collection of fables from 17 fabulists including Aesop, Bidpai, the Hitopadeśa, Krylov, La Fontaine, and Carlos Yriarte, and from Malaya, Africa, China, and England. Charles Curry, in his *Children's Literature* (Chicago [1927]), calls it "the best general collection from all fields, including both the folk fable and the modern literary fable."

No notes as to sources are provided, but a brief introduction sketches the travels and migrations of the fables.

105 Daugherty, James. ANDY AND THE LION. New York, Viking, 1938. 78 p. 28 cm.

PZ7.D2625An

☆   The story in this modern picture book with Daugherty's vigorous drawings is a near relative of Aesop's "Lion and the Mouse," and even closer to "Androcles and the Lion."

106 Aesopus. AESOP'S FABLES, a new version written by Munro Leaf, with illustrations by Robert Lawson. New York, Heritage Press [c1941] 134 p. 26.5 cm.

PA3855.E5L35

☆   A colloquial retelling of 101 fables for young children, with conversations often added. The morals, which have often been changed, sometimes miss the point. Humorous, rustic illustrations, some full page.

107 Aulaire, Ingri (Mortenson) d', *and* Edgar P. d'Aulaire. DON'T COUNT YOUR CHICKS. Garden City, N.Y., Doubleday, Doran, 1943. [40] p. 31 cm.

PZ7.A914Do

Illustration by James Daugherty from his Andy and the Lion. *Copyright © 1938*
The Viking Press; reproduced by permission. *(Item 105)*

☆ In this version for young children with full-page lithographs (half in color) by the D'Aulaires, the milkmaid with her pail of milk has become an old woman with a basket of eggs.

108 Aesopus. AESOP'S FABLES, from the translations of Thomas James and George Tyler Townsend; introduction by Angelo Patri; illustrated by Glen Rounds. Philadelphia, Lippincott [1949] 162 p. (Lippincott classics)   PZ8.2.A254Jam2

☆ Notable for excellence of typographical layout and design. The first word or two of each fable, printed in capitals and in color, suggests medieval manuscripts and creates an interest in the text. Small, colorful crayon drawings.

109 Chaucer, Geoffrey. CHANTICLEER AND THE FOX. Adapted and illustrated by Barbara Cooney. New York, Crowell [1958] [31] p. 27 cm.   PZ8.2.C47Ch

☆ A prose adaptation taken from the Lumiansky translation of Chaucer's "Nun's Priest's Tale," which in turn is an adaptation of the Aesopic fable "The Cock and the Fox."

Handsomely illustrated in colored scratchboard drawings with medieval details like those in old manuscripts.

Illustration by Barbara Cooney from Chaucer's Chanticleer and the Fox. *Copyright © 1958 by Thomas Y. Crowell Company; reproduced by permission. (Item 109)*

110 Aesopus. THE MILLER, HIS SON, AND THEIR DONKEY. Illustrated by Roger Duvoisin. New York, Whittlesey House [1962] 30 p. 26 cm.

PZ8.2.A254Du

☆ These humorous illustrations are typical of Duvoisin—brush drawings with purple and green wash; French peasant costumes and scenes as background. The version here is that used by Artzybasheff, but with the ending softened—the miller *almost* loses his donkey.

111 Evans, Katherine. THE MICE THAT ATE IRON. Chicago, A. Whitman [1963] [32] p. 25 cm.

PZ8.2.E92Mi

☆ An example of a single fable produced for use with young children, told in easy style, with large print and bright and colorful pictures.

112 Aesopus. AESOP'S FABLES. Selected and adapted by Louis Untermeyer. Illustrated by A. and M. Provensen. New York, Golden Press [°1965] 92 p. 31 cm.

PZ8.2.A254Un

☆ A modern approach in both text and illustrations. Lively colors splashed all over the large pages in humorous drawings depict dressed-up animals in comical caricatures. Sly or coy asides emerge from the characters' mouths in the pictures.

Studies

113 VITA AESOPI. Ex vratislaviensi ac partim monacensi et vindobonensi codicibus nunc primum edidit Antonius Westermann. Brunswick, sumptum fecit Georgius Westermann, 1845. viii, 59 p.

PA3851.A4 1845

☆ The Life of Aesop, in Greek, is based on three early manuscripts. Westermann was the first and only modern scholar (before Perry) to publish the Life of Aesop based on manuscripts earlier than Planudes. This version, now a rare book, is analyzed in detail by Perry in *Studies in the Text History and Fables of Aesop* (item 119).

114 Aesopus. STEINHÖWELS ASOP; herausgegeben von Hermann Österley. Tübingen, Litterarischer verein in Stuttgart, 1873. 372 p. (Bibliothek des Litterarischen vereins in Stuttgart, [bd.] 117)

PT1101.L5, v. 117

This is a reprint of the text of the original edition printed about 1477 by J. Zainer in Ulm. Steinhöwel collected and translated the Life of Aesop (of Remicius from Planudes), and the fables of Romulus (main part of the text), and of Remicius, Avianus, Petrus Alphonsi, and Poggius. The German translation, which seems primitive now, with its 15th-century spelling, follows immediately after the Latin of each fable. Steinhöwel gave a subject index, by moral, at the end, probably for the use of the fables in sermons, a common practice in the Middle Ages.

Österley, in the introduction, gives the background of the translation and emphasizes its importance as the first printed version in Europe—the French translation of 1484 by Macho, the 1484 English of Caxton, the Dutch of 1485, the Czech of 1487, the Spanish of 1489, and later editions were all based on it.

115 —— The fables of Aesop, as first printed by William Caxton in 1484, with those of Avian, Alfonso and Poggio, now again edited and induced by Joseph Jacobs. London, D. Nutt, 1889. 2 v. (283, 322 p.) (Bibliothèque de Carabas series) PA3855.E5C3 1889

Volume 1, *History of the Aesopic Fable,* includes a diagram of "The Pedigree of Caxton's Aesop," which is most helpful. This study, based on earlier French and German research, compares the later versions of Aesop derived from Phaedrus' verse ("Our Aesop is Phaedrus with Trimmings"), tracing back through him and the Greek of Babrius and on into Greek folklore. He relates the whole body of Greek fable to that of India and compares many parallel stories. He also discusses the fable collections of the Middle Ages. The frontispiece shows three scenes from the Bayeux tapestry depicting Aesop fables.

In a summary section Jacobs concludes that only two nations, India and Greece, independently, shaped the beast tale to teach moral truths by means of the true fable. Until the 1940's, when several important studies were done at the University of Illinois under the direction of Ben E. Perry, this was the only elaborate and scholarly study in English, and it is still the most readable.

Volume 2 is a reprint of the Caxton edition of 1484, in the original spelling with reproductions of the primitive woodcuts. Glossary, p. 319–322.

116 Hervieux, Léopold. Les fabulistes latins depuis le siècle d' Auguste jusqu'à la fin du moyen âge. Paris, Firmin-Didot, 1893–99. 5 v. PA6135.F3H4

Contents.—t. 1–2. Phèdre et ses anciens imitateurs.—t. 3. Avianus et ses anciens imitateurs.—t. 4. Études de Cheriton et ses dérivés.— t. 5. Jean de Capoue et ses dérivés.

This monumental work is valuable especially for the detailed descriptions of the manuscripts—many of them previously unknown— of the works of Phaedrus, Romulus (in several versions which include Vincent de Beauvais, Walter of England, and Marie de France), Avianus, and others. Hervieux established relationships of manuscripts (revealing which one was copied from which) and discovered a significant number of manuscripts for the Romulus (the most popular of the medieval versions). He lists all known editions of these many versions.

117 Aesopus. YSOPET-AVIONNET: the Latin and French texts edited by Kenneth McKenzie and William A. Oldfather. [Urbana] University of Illinois, 1919. 286 p. (University of Illinois studies in language and literature, v. 5, no. 4) PA8230.W3 1919

☆ The first complete publication of this manuscript edition of 64 fables of Aesop and 18 fables of Avianus in Latin and Old French. The Aesopic fables are, with a few exceptions, derived from the paraphrase of Romulus in distichs known as *Aesopus Moralisatus,* ascribed by some authorities to Walter of England.

The text consists of a collection of Aesopic fables in Latin verse, with a 14th-century French translation, based on three closely related 14th-century manuscripts preserved at Brussels, London, and Paris, which are described and compared in detail in the lengthy introduction. The editors point out that they have reproduced on 12 plates "from the rotary prints (hence white on black), and on a somewhat reduced scale, the complete series of illustrations which appeared in P [the Paris manuscript] together with a few characteristic selections from the series in B and L [the Brussels and London manuscripts]."

118 Hower, Charles C. STUDIES ON THE SO-CALLED ACCURSIANA RECENSION of the life and fables of Aesop. Urbana, Ill., 1936. 8 p. PA3858.H6 1936

Abstract of thesis (Ph. D.), University of Illinois, 1936.

Analysis of the Accursiana recension of the Life and Fables ascribed to Maximus Planudes, published by Bonus Accursius at Milan about 1480 (item 59). The author compares this manuscript in such matters as style, syntax, and shortening of words with a genuine work of Planudes—namely his Letters. Because of striking linguistic resemblances, he concludes that Planudes was indeed the redactor of the Accursiana texts, dating from the early 14th century.

119 Perry, Ben E. STUDIES IN THE TEXT HISTORY OF THE LIFE AND FABLES OF AESOP. Haverford, Pa., American Philological Association, 1936. xvi, 240 p. (Philological monographs, no. 7) PA3858.P4

☆ "I propose to define," Mr. Perry says (p. vii), ". . . the broad outlines of the Aesopic tradition insofar as it relates to the commonly received texts of the Life and Fables, and to the hitherto unknown but very important representatives thereof which are contained in manuscript 397 of the Pierpont Morgan library," which probably dates from about 980 to 1050.

A very detailed and scholarly study of the Life of Aesop, "one of the few genuinely popular books that have come down from ancient times," and of the Fables. Part 1 consists of a textual comparison of the Life as given in Pierpont Morgan manuscript 397 with Westermann's version and of the complete text of four corresponding papyrus fragments. In part 2, a long table (p. 82–145) compares the Morgan manuscript of 238 fables with other old (Class I) manuscripts line by line, giving all the variant readings of the Morgan manuscript that seemed noteworthy. Perry discusses the relations of the various .manuscripts and describes the fables in each manuscript.

The archetype of the Morgan manuscript he dates as probably from the second century A.D.; the Westermann Life is based on five later manuscripts. On p. 229–230 he gives a summary table of successive recensions, the approximate dates of origin, and sources of the Life and of the Fables. Plates show six of the manuscripts analyzed.

The famous manuscript 397 also contains parts of three stories from *Kalīlah wa-Dimnah,* in a Greek version, not that of Symeon Seth. It was identified by Elinor Husselman of the Pierpont Morgan Library and described by her in 1939 (London, Christophers. PA5303. B5 1939). Six plates of facsimiles show several of the illustrations from this manuscript.

120 Aesopus. AESOPICA; a series of texts relating to Aesop or ascribed to him or closely connected with the literary tradition that bears his name. Collected and critically edited, in part translated from Oriental languages, with a commentary and historical essay, by Ben E. Perry. v. 1. Urbana, University of Illinois Press, 1952. 765 p.

PA3851.A2 1952

A monumental study, incorporating the results of years of critical research. The first volume of a projected work of three or four volumes, this consists of the Greek and Latin texts, including the first publication of the Life of Aesop in the Pierpont Morgan manuscript 397.

Perry's original project was simply to prepare a critical edition of the Life of Aesop in the older and more complete but little known version of this anecdotal biography, which was published for the first and only time by Westermann in 1845, now a rare book. Perry discovered that the Morgan manuscript was a long lost treasure from Frascati, missing since about 1798, and that it was 200 years older than any used by Westermann.

Here the editor has "tried to put before the reader . . . the substance, though not the various forms . . . of everything ascribed to Aesop or said about him in Greek literature down to the fall of Constantinople, and in Latin literature through Romulus, together with all the different fables, whether ascribed to Aesop or not, which were plainly regarded by the ancients as 'Aesopic.'" This material consists of 471 Greek fables and 725 Latin with notes of sources and dates. The indexes enable the reader to identify a certain fable or motif, and the comparative table gives the number of the fable in each of six other collections or editions: the Halm, Chambry, and Hausrath editions, and the Babrius, Phaedrus, and Avianus versions.

The Accursiana recension, edited and stylized by Planudes, was omitted to make room for older versions of the same traditional material.

The main body of Aesopic fables is from the collection made by Phaedrus, a Greek slave freed by Augustus in the first century A.D. He put the earlier Greek prose fables, about 200, into Latin iambics.

In the Middle Ages many variations and additions were made in the collection, notably the prose version ascribed to Romulus in the ninth century. After the invention of printing, Phaedrus' collection became the basis for textbook editions of Aesop's fables, his iambic verses being favorite materials for the teaching of Latin to schoolboys. Hundreds of editions of Phaedrus were published, with and without translations.

Definitive modern editions in Latin with scholarly notes are those of Louis Havet, *Phaedri Avgvsti Liberti Fabulae Aesopiae* (Paris, Hachette, 1895. PA6563.A2 1895); Domenico Bassi, *Phaedri Fabvlae*) Augustae Taurinorum in aedibus I. B. Paraviae et sociorum [1918] PA6105.C6P45); and John Percival Postgate, *Phaedri Fabulae Aesopiae* (Oxford, Clarendoniano [1919] PA6563.A2 1919).

121 Phaedrus. PHAEDRI, AUGUSTI CAESARIS LIBERTI, Fabularum Aesopiarum libri V; notis perpetuis illustrati, & cum integris aliorum observationibus in lucem editi à Johanne Laurentio. Index omnium vocabulorum. Amstelodami, Johannem Janssonium à Waesberge, 1667. 2 v.   PA6563.A2 1667

☆   The first volume contains a Life of Phaedrus and the Latin text, with many notes, comparisons with other versions such as Avianus, Modestis, and Doni, a Greek version, and commentaries. The many clear and pleasing engravings show a busy city life of medieval times. The frontispiece (signed Chr. Hagens, Sculp) is of Augustus with Phaedrus and Aesop before him.

Volume 2 includes the Laurentius Index Vocabulorum and the Index Rerum & Verborum, which indexes the notes as well as the text, both Greek and Latin.

122 ——— PHAEDRI AUG. LIBERTI FABULARUM AESOPIARUM libri quinque; item fabulae quaedam ex ms. veteri à Marquardo Gudio descriptae; cum indice vocum & locutionum. Appendicis loco adjiciuntur fabulae greacae quaedam & latinae ex variis authoribus collectae; quas claudit Avieni Aesopicarum fabularum liber unicus. Londini, ex officinâ Jacobi Tonson & Johannis Watts, 1713. 60, [115] p.

PA6563.A2 1713

☆   The preface states that the editor, Michael Maittaire, has here presented "a compleat *Collection* of all the Greek and Latin authors . . . with compleat Indexes." The "Index in Phaedrum" is that of Marquard Gude.

The frontispiece shows Aesop in the background dictating his fables to Phaedrus. The title page is printed in red and black; decorated initials, headpieces and tailpieces add further illustration.

123 ———— Phèdre, traduit en français par J.-B. Gail. A Paris, De l'imprimerie de Delance. L'an v. 1796. 280 p. (Les trois fabulistes [t. 2])   PN984.G3, t. 2

The French prose translation of Jean-Baptiste Gail appears on the pages opposite the Latin metrical version of Phaedrus. The notes of Brottier are included, with additional grammatical notes by the translator, p. 166-259. Pages 271-274 contain a list of editions of Phaedrus from 1596 to 1783.

124 ———— Phaedri Augusti liberti Fabularum Aesopiarum libri v., ad codices mss. et optimas editiones recognovit, varietatem lectionis et commentarium perpetuum adjecit Joann. Gottlob. Sam. Schwabe. Accedunt Romuli Fabularum Aesopiarum libri IV. ad codicem divionensem et perantiquam editionem ulmensem nunc primum emendata et notis illustrati. Cum tabulis aeri incisis. Brunsvigae, sumto F. Viewegii, 1806. 2 v. (608, 696 p.)   PA6563.A2 1806

☆ Each book is preceded by an engraved halftitle, with vignette.

"Aesthetische bemerkungen über die Fabeln des Phaedrus vom herrn professor Jacobs" (preceded by halftitle in Latin): vol. I, p. [239]-262.

Volume 1 contains a Life of Phaedrus, a "Literary Notice" listing all known manuscripts and editions of Phaedrus, and books 1 and 2 of the Fables. Volume 2 includes books 3 to 5 of the Fables and an index to Phaedrus. The text is entirely in Latin.

The fables are complete, with notes on variations filling most of each page. Additions and emendations come from *Magasin Encyclopédique* and other sources. The work of Babrius, Aphthonius, Romulus, Anonymous Neveleti, Anonymous Nilanti, and others is also discussed.

125 ———— Phaedri liberti Aügusti Fabulae. Nova editio, selectis P. Desbillons Fabellis, notis gallicis et prosodiæ signis adornata. Lugduni, J. B. Pelagaud et socii; Parisiis, Vᵉ Poussielgue-Rusand, 1852. 1 p. l., [vii]-viii, 114 p.   PA6563.A2 1852

☆ A typical little 19th-century school edition. The copy exhibited shows evidence of diligent use.

126 ———— Romulus: Die paraphrasen des Phaedrus und die Aesopische fabel in mittelalter, von Herman Oesterley. Berlin, Weidmann, 1870. xxxvii, [38]-124 p.   PA6565.A1 1870

Romulus is essentially a prose rendering of Phaedrus. Oesterley, a pioneering German scholar, treats this version from a philological viewpoint and for its importance in literary history. He compares several medieval manuscripts, including Codex Burneianus, Marie de France, and Steinhöwel's Romulus.

127   Aesopus. DER LATEINISCHE ÄSOP DES ROMULUS UND DIE PROSA-FASSUNGEN DES PHÄEDRUS: kritischer text mit kommentar und einleitenden untersuchungen von Georg Thiele. Heidelberg, C. Winter, 1910. ccxxxviii, 360 p.   PA3852.R6 1910

Romulus—"the only large fable collection in Latin prose from antiquity"—contains 100 pieces. Thiele mentions the work of Oesterley and Hervieux and goes on to analyze the important recensions as to style and content—which fables are pure Phaedrus and which "contaminated"—the Ur-form of the Phaedrus. A list of the Phaedrus in the Romulus-corpus follows. A table gives a brief outline of the contents of seven important versions. There are three plates of illustrations from manuscripts and early printed *Aesops* at the end of the book.

In "The Tradition of the Romulus-corpus" Thiele discusses the five versions which he compares in the main part of the book. In four columns across the two pages he gives the texts of these five versions of the Romulus, with detailed notes of other variations and with more general notes in German at the bottom of the page. The versions treated are: Recensio gallicana, Recensio de Kodex W (Wolfenbuttel), Recensio vetus, Phädrus-Text nach Havets Ausgabe, and Phädrus-Auflösungen in Kodex Ademar.

128   Adams, F. B., Jr. THE CODEX PITHOEANUS OF PHRAEDRUS. *In* Horn book magazine, v. 41, June 1965: 260–266.   Z1037.A1A15, v. 41

The Codex Pithoeanus, a ninth-century copy of an earlier classical manuscript, is the earliest known surviving manuscript of Phaedrus. It was discovered in September 1596 by François Pithon, who presented it to his brother Pierre. Its history and description are given in detail in Hervieux's *Les Fabulistes Latins* (item 116), v. 1, p. 38–68. The manuscript was purchased recently by the Pierpont Morgan Library and became the centerpiece for an exhibit there of Aesop fables in January–February 1965. F. B. Adams, Jr., the director of the library, gave this history of the book and the circumstances of its acquisition at the opening of the exhibition, in an address which was printed in the *Horn Book Magazine*.

BABRIUS

Valerius Babrius was a Roman who probably lived in the third century A.D. He may have made his translation of some 200 fables, from Latin into Greek verse, in connection with his duties as tutor to a son of Alexander Severus (ca. A.D. 235).

The standard definitive edition in Greek with Latin notes and commentary is that of Crusius (item 132).

129 Babrius. BABRII FABULAE IAMBICAE CXXI. Joh. Fr. Boissonade recensuit. 2. ed. novis curis exploita. Paris, Firmin Didot fratres, 1844. 67 p. PA3941.A2 1844

The main body of Babrian fables was first published in 1844 from the manuscript discovered in 1843 by Manoides Minas in the monastery of Sainte-Laure at Mount Athos. This second edition, of the same year, contains corrections of the first edition which are pointed out by the editor and omits two fables in the first.

130 [Egger, Émile] EXAMEN DES NOUVELLES FABLES DE BABRIUS découvertes en Grèce par m. Minoïde Minas, et publiées . . . par m. Boissonade. [Paris, Imprimenie de P. Dupont et cⁱᵉ, 1844?] 16 p. PA3941.Z5E3

A review of *Babrii fabulae iambicae CXXIII*, edited by Boissonade and published by Firmin Didot, Paris, 1844. Found in 1843 in the monastery of Sainte-Laure at Mount Athos, the manuscript was an important discovery. It represents one of the latest redactions of Babrius and has suffered alterations at the hands of later interpolators.

131 Babrius. BABRIUS; edited with introductory dissertations, critical notes, commentary, and lexicon by W. Gunion Rutherford. London, Macmillan, 1883. ciii, 202 p. (Scriptores fabularum graeci, v. 1) PA3941.A2 1883

Of the four introductory studies to this definitive text of Babrius, the first relates him to Latin verse although he was writing in Greek, during the reign of Alexander Severus; the second gives a history of the Greek fable; the third treats the language of Babrius; and the fourth the history of the text.

The introductory chapter on "The History of Greek Fable" is especially valuable. Rutherford concludes that "there seem to be no data by which to determine the ultimate source of fable or the primitive form of any particular apologue which is not merely literary." He believes the Greek fables to be at least as old as the Indian.

The mythiambics of the text itself, p. 3-131, are fully annotated with notes in both Latin and English. Pages 135-192 consist of a Greek lexicon of words used by Babrius.

132 ———— BABRII FABVLAE AESOPEAE. Recognovit prolegomenis et indicibvs instrvxit Otto Crvsivs; accedvnt fabvlarvm dactylicarvm et iambicarvm reliqviae. Ignatii et aliorvm tetrasticha iambica recensita a Carolo Friderico Mveller. Leipzig, in aedibvs B. G. Tevbneri, 1897. xcv, 440 p. 3 fold. facsim. (Bibliotheca scriptorum graecorum et romanorum Teubneriana). PA3404.B2 1897

The standard critical edition of Babrian Fables which includes all the mythiambics and many fragments as well, with many detailed notes. The introduction treats Babrius' metrical art and his dialectic, and previous studies and editions, including Rutherford's.

133 ———— AESOP'S FABLES, told by Valerius Babrius. Translated by Denison B. Hull. Decorations by Rainey Bennett. [Chicago] University of Chicago Press [1960] [116] p.   PA3941.E5   1960

☆   The translator's preface gives a short historical account of the versions of the fables. He considers Babrius the best; "colorful and imaginative and, altogether more representative of the Greek spirit of fable." The rhymed verse translation is lively, light, clever; from the Greek text of Gunion Rutherford of Balliol College, Oxford, 1883. The little blue drawings of animals are charming but are not placed near the fable they illustrate.

AVIANUS

134   Avianus, Flavius. THE FABLES OF AVIANUS, edited, with prolegomena, critical apparatus, commentary, excursus, and index by Robinson Ellis. Oxford, Clarendon Press, 1887.   151 p.   PA6225.A2   1887

In the prolegomena Ellis discusses the person and dates of Avianus, as well as his prosody, diction, and syntax, with full use of notes and examples. Since the preface to the fables is inscribed to Theodosius Macrobius, author of the *Saturnalia,* Ellis concludes that Avianus may be the young Avianus or Avienus in that work; and further that because the banquet on which it is based took place somewhere between 367 and 385 A.D. (although it was not published until about 400 or 420), Avianus must have written his fables before 385. Avianus wrote a Latin version of the Greek poetic text of Babrius. Ellis considers the style of Avianus to have some merits but to be far inferior to Babrius and even to Phaedrus.

Ellis describes the seven important manuscripts on which Avianus based his text. He notes differences in the manuscripts and provides an elaborate commentary, p. 49–130, and a comparison with the Greek of Babrius.

135   Oldfather, William A. BIBLIOGRAPHICAL NOTES ON THE FABLES OF AVIANUS.   *In* Bibliographical Society of America. Papers v. 15, pt. 2, 1921: 61–72.   Z1008.B51P, v. 15, pt. 2

W. A. Oldfather of the University of Illinois gives a list of editions and translations unknown to Hervieux (see item 116, vol. 3), additional data on some imperfectly described by him, and a few notes on some books in American libraries that he visited. He notes that "a systematic bibliography of Avianus should include all the editions and translations of Steinhöwel's famous Aesop as well as those of the Latin prose version" (p. 72). His descriptions are complete and explicit and include several Steinhöwels.

136 Bedrick, Theodore. THE PROSE ADAPTATIONS OF AVIANUS. Urbana, Ill., 1940. 4 p.   PA6225.Z5B4 1940

137 Hale, Clarence B. THE TEXT TRADITION OF THE AESOPIC FABLES belonging to the so-called Augustana recension. Urbana, Ill., 1941. 5 p. diagr.   PA3858.H3

138 Jones, William R. THE TEXT TRADITION OF AVIANUS. Urbana, Ill., 1940. 7 p. diagr.   PA6225.Z5J6 1940

"My aim has been the classification, and in part also the evaluation, of the mss. of Avianus" (p. [1]).

139 Ryan, Eileen P. THE VERSE ADAPTATIONS OF AVIANUS. Part 1. The Astensis and its derivatives. Urbana, Ill., 1940 [5] p.
                                                      PA6225.Z5R8 1940

The above entries describe abstracts of studies on Avianus which were done as doctoral dissertations at the University of Illinois about 1940 under the direction of B. E. Perry and William Oldfather.

140 Goldschmidt, Adolph. AN EARLY MANUSCRIPT OF THE AESOP FABLES OF AVIANUS and related manuscripts. Princeton, Princeton University Press, 1947. 63 p. (Studies in manuscript illumination, no. 1)
                                                           ND3395.A35G6

☆ A study of book illumination in southern France, based on a Carolingian manuscript in the Bibliothèque Nationale (ms. lat. nouv. acq. 1132) showing the development of illustrations for Aesop's fables in Gothic manuscripts from the 6th to the 15th centuries.

Sixty-one facsimiles of medieval manuscripts appear here with their illustrations, each introduced and described in the documented text. Several fables are represented numerous times, allowing comparison of the illustrations. The Bayeux tapestry, the fable collections of Vincent of Beauvais and Marie de France, and the Ysopet and Avionnet are discussed.

MARIE DE FRANCE

141 Marie de France. DIE FABELN DER MARIE DE FRANCE. Mit benutzung des von Ed. Mall hinterlassenen materials, herausgegeben von Karl Warnke. Halle, M. Niemeyer, 1898. xiii, cxlvi, 447 p. (Biblioteca normannica, v. 6)   PC2931.B5

Karl Warnke's is the definitive edition of the 102 Aesopic fables of Marie de France. A long introduction gives background and criticism; to the complete text he adds detailed notes on sources and variations in the many manuscripts he used, and a glossary of Marie's 12th-century vocabulary.

142 ——— FABLES, selected and edited by A. Ewert and R. C. Johnston. Oxford, B. Blackwell, 1942. xxi, 88 p. (Blackwell's French texts)
PQ1494.F2 1942

Marie made her collection of fables in the late 12th century, sometime after 1189. She states that her work is based on an English collection, translated from a Latin original by a certain Alvrez. Comparison with extant Latin versions of fables shows the first 40 fables in Marie's complete collection to be based upon the *Romulus Nilantii* (first published by F. Nilant as *Romuli Fabulae Aesopicae* at Leyden in 1709), a prose derivative of the fourth-century *Romulus;* to these were added some fables taken from the vulgate *Romulus,* some stories taken from the *Renart* tales, and others based on popular fabliaux or monks' tales.

Pages 66–88 include notes and glossary to the text.

143 Joly, Aristide. MARIE DE FRANCE ET LES FABLES AU MOYEN-AGE. Caën, Legost-Clérisse, 1863. 65 p. PQ1494.F7J7

A study of the fables of Marie de France and their applications—the mores and society represented in them—which also speculates as to her identity and that of Guillaume, her protector.

La Fontaine

LA FONTAINE

La Fontaine is so important in France that he has been compared with Homer and Shakespeare: "Un Homère en raccourci, cela va sans dire, un Shakespeare en miniature" says Georges Lafenestre in his study (item 167), p. 149. No English writer has ever equaled La Fontaine as a fabulist although many have used the fable form; his retellings in verse with new inventions give them the position of a major literary monument.

French children learn La Fontaine fables almost as early as our children know Mother Goose and they acquire during elementary school a thorough knowledge of the verse of the fables.

Jean de la Fontaine was born in Chateau Thierry in 1621. He went to Paris to school and later to make his literary and social career. The first collection of fables, comprising books 1 to 6, was published in 1668. Most of the fables were based on Phaedrus, or the prose version of Romulus; others on various books of Emblems, which were popular medieval works, long poems with woodcuts, and on other French writers. In preparing the fables for publication La Fontaine obtained the services of François Chauveau, who had illustrated one of his earlier works. His vignettes are much like those in Nevelet's collection of Phaedrus and in various emblem books.

The second collection was published in 5 books in 1678, and the sources for many of these fables are found in the *Fables de Pilpay* or *Livre des Lumières*. Book 12, published 15 years later, includes some fables previously published in various journals. Dedicated to Le Duc de Burgogne, grandson of Louis XIV, it contains fables on themes suggested to the boy by his teacher Fénelon. La Fontaine died in Paris in 1695.

As early as 1699 some of La Fontaine's fables were translated into English in the "Supplement of Fables" to Roger L'Estrange's collection which first appeared in 1692 (item 86). In 1703 Bernard de Mandeville wrote *Some Fables After the Easie and Familiar Method of M. de la Fontaine,* of which there is a copy at the Bodleian. Translations of single fables appeared in various magazines. In 1761 Baskerville printed for R & J Dodsley *Select Fables of Aesop and Other Fabulists* (item 87), which included 10 of La Fontaine's. The first verse translation was that of Robert Thompson in 1806, *La Fontaine's Fables* (item 151).

The various styles of illustration for La Fontaine's fables are well represented in the Library of Congress. A copy of the 1668 first edition containing the illustrations of Chauveau was presented by Mr. Rosenwald in 1964. The important illustrator of the 18th century was Oudry, whose work appeared from 1755 to 1759. Duvivier's typical 18th-century engravings were published in installments from 1784 to 1787; Grandville's caricatures appeared in 1838. The dark, murky groups of animals by Doré, first published in 1868, are represented in the Library by the combined edition of

1873. The Library also has Calder's marvelous free line and witty new approach of 1948, and finally Chagall's superb set of etchings, done in 1952.

Editions of the Fables

144 La Fontaine, Jean de. FABLES CHOISIES. Mises en vers par M. de la Fontaine. A Paris, Chez Claude Barbin, 1668. 284 p.

Rosenwald Coll

☆   The original quarto edition of the first collection of fables, containing the first six books, illustrated by François Chauveau and bound by Cuzin, was presented to the Library in 1964 by Lessing J. Rosenwald.

145 ——— FABLES CHOISIES. Mises en vers par Monsieur de La Fontaine, et par luy reveuës, corrigées, & augmentées de nouveau. Suivant la copie imprimée à Paris. La Haye, H. van Bulderen, 1688. 4 pt. in 1 v. 16 cm.   PQ1808.A1   1688

☆   A small volume, including 11 books of fables (the 12th was not published until 1693), this is a counterfeit of the van Dunewalt edition published in Anvers in the same year. The vignettes engraved by Henri Cause imitate those of François Chauveau of the Barbin Thierry edition of 1678, which are the same for the first book as the original edition of 1668. The printing of the text and the plates is clear and distinct.

146 ——— FABLES CHOISIES. Mises en vers par Monsieur de La Fontaine. Et par lui revuës, corrigées & augmentées de nouveau. Amsterdam, Z. Chatelain, 1727–28. 5 pt. in 3 v. 16 cm.

PQ1808.A1   1728

"La vie d'Ésope le Phrygien" (based on the "Vita Aesopi" wrongly ascribed to Planudes): pt. 1, p. [17–38].

The first four parts of this full collection are reprinted from the van Dunewalt edition of 1688 with the same illustrations, by Henri Cause, and an added frontispiece showing La Fontaine surrounded by the Muses, cherubs, Aesop, and various animals. (The plate on p. 13 is upside down.) The fifth part contains 32 engravings, copies of Cause, but not signed. This volume includes two pieces not usually admitted to the published fables of La Fontaine: "La Fleuve Scamandre" and "L'Hymenée et l'Amour," which are really pastorales. The illustration of Daphnis and Alcimadure is repeated at the head of "L'Amour Vangé."

147 ——— FABLES CHOISIES, mises en vers par J. de La Fontaine. Paris, Desaint & Saillant, Imprimerie de C.-A. Jombert, 1755–59.

4 v.   45 cm.   PQ1801.A1   1755   Rare Bk

☆   Edited by C. P. de Monthenault d'Égly.

The outstanding edition of the 18th century, this La Fontaine contains 276 plates engraved by Cochin and other noted engravers, after drawings by J. B. Oudry. They depict the fables in rich, Regency settings. Several of the fables have more than one illustration. There are also 209 tailpieces engraved by Lesueur and Papillon after Bachellier and an engraved portrait of Oudry after N. de Lergillière.

Oudry took 5 years to prepare his drawings. Cochin retouched them for engraving and in 1756 exhibited the collection of the originals.

148   ———— FABLES CHOISIES, mises en vers par J. de La Fontaine. Nouv. éd. gravée en taille-douce, les figures par le S^r. Fessard, le texte par le S^r. Montulay. Dédiées aux Enfans de France. Paris [Fessard] 1765-75. 6 v.   PQ1808.A1   1765   Rosenwald Coll

☆   An edition containing 238 fables, illustrated with 245 engravings and 473 flower-vignettes and tailpieces after drawings by Bardin, Bidault, Loutherbourg, Monnet, and others, engraved by Étienne Fessard. Although not outstanding as to text, printing, or engravings, this edition was financed by subscription.

An "Eloge historique de M. de La Fontaine par M. l'abbé d'Olivet" appears in volume 1, p. li–lxviii. As the first life, it includes most of the legends that formed the basis for later biographies.

149   ———— LES FIGURES DES FABLES DE LA FONTAINE, gravées par Simon et Coiny, d'après les dessins du s^r. J^{ce}. Vivier. Paris, Simon et Coiny [1784-87?] 46 pts. in 4 cases. 27 cm.

NE650.D84A44   Rosenwald Coll

☆   The illustrations, issued in parts, were prepared for the 6-volume edition printed by Didot in Paris in 1787. Parts 1–9 include engraved text for the first 88 pages; the completed edition, however, had printed text throughout in a neat, small, italic type.

The 46 parts were issued in monthly installments and sold by subscription, 300 having been ordered in advance, another 200 being for sale. Each installment contained six engravings typical of the late 18th century by Ignace Duvivier.

150   ———— FABLES DE LA FONTAINE, avec les notes de Chamfort. A Paris, De l'imprimerie de Delance, 1796. 2 v. (260, 364 p.) (Les trois fabulists. [t. 3–4])   PN984.G3, t. 3–4

Volume 3 contains a 50-page life of La Fontaine and the important *Éloge de La Fontaine* by Sébastien Chamfort, first published in 1774, which gives a brilliant comparison of La Fontaine and Molière. Chamfort sketches the character of La Fontaine against the background of his time, and his notes (in both volumes) provide personal commentary and criticism of the language and versification but do not give sources.

151 ———— LA FONTAINE'S FABLES. Now first translated from the French by Robert Thomson. Paris, Sold by Chenu, 1806. 4 v. in 2.

PQ1811.E3T5

"A sketch of La Fontaine's life and character" is contained in volume 1, p. 1–13, and "A sketch of Aesop's life from Croxall" in volume 2, p. 1–22.

The first translation into English verse (earlier versions existed in prose), this is lively, although not always succinct. It includes La Fontaine's preface and an introduction by the translator.

152 ———— FABLES INÉDITES DES XIIe, XIIIe ET XIVe SIÈCLES, et Fables de La Fontaine, rapprochées de celles de tous les auteurs qui avoient, avant lui, traité les mêmes sujets, précédées d'une notice sur les fabulistes, par A. C. M. Robert. Ornées d'un portrait de La Fontaine, de 90 gravures en taille-douce, et de 4 fac-similé. Paris, É. Cabin, 1825. 2 v. cclxij, 368, 604 p.

PQ1808.A1 1825

☆ Robert has searched through all the old authors and editions of fables for those that La Fontaine used in his *Fables Choisies*. His long introduction (vol. 1, p. xiii–ccxi) gives brief biographical information on many of the authors and compilers beginning with the Greek.

This edition of La Fontaine includes medieval French and Latin fables heretofore unpublished, notably the collections, entitled by the editor "Yzopet I," "Yzopet-Avionnet," and "Yzopet II," which are respectively based on the paraphrase of Romulus by the Anonymus Neveleti, the fables of Avianus, and the *Aesopus Novus* by Alexander Neckam. These have been inserted at the end of each corresponding fable of La Fontaine. The "Appendice" (vol. 2, p. [445]–576) contains the fables of Yzopet I and II for which no parallels exist, and the "Romulus Bibliothecae regiae" ("Romulus Roberti"), 22 fables in Latin prose, 18 of which are based on the fables of Marie de France.

The plates, engraved by Paul Legrand, are reproductions of the 85 miniatures in "Yzopet I," manuscript 1595 of the Bibliothèque Nationale. They include "Facsimilé des premiers vers du manuscrit" and 5 additional miniatures, numbered in duplicate, reproduced from manuscripts of *Le Roman du Renard* and of "Yzopet II."

"Notice des principales éditions des Fables et des oeuvres de Jean de La Fontaine, par m. Barbier" (vol. 2, p. [563]–576).

153 ———— FABLES DE LA FONTAINE, illustrées par J. J. Grandville. Nouv. éd. Paris, H. Fournier aîné, 1838. 2 v. (292, 312 p.)

PQ1808.A1 1838 Rare Bk

☆ "La vie d'Ésope le Phrygien," based on the "Vita Aesopi" wrongly ascribed to Planudes, appears in volume 1, p. [xiii]–xxviii.

Grandville's effective wood engravings show elaborately garbed people and amusingly dressed animals. These include small designs above the titles, around the fable numbers, a frontispiece showing a bust of La Fontaine supported by two elephants, ornate title pages for each of the separate books, and 120 full-page illustrations for the fables themselves. Grandville (pseudonym for Jean Ignace Isidore Gérard) was a caricaturist who often depicted humans in the guise of animals; here he shows animals behaving like humans. Taine thought these illustrations spoiled La Fontaine and considered them a "vulgar carnival."

This "nouvelle édition" shows some differences from the first, also 1838, in the decorations; furthermore, it omits "L'Hymenée et l'Amour."

154 ———— FABLES OF LA FONTAINE. Illustrated by J. J. Grandville. Translated from the French, by Elizur Wright, Jr. 2d ed. Boston, E. Wright, Jr.; New York, W. A. Coleman, 1841. 2 v. [489, 654] p. 23 cm. PQ1811.E3W6 1841

☆ A preface notes La Fontaine's indebtedness in the first six books to Phaedrus—"the same curious condensations." Wright has based his Life of La Fontaine on Robert Thompson's. The English translation of the fables, printed on leaves separate from the French version, is interleaved with the French of 1838. It comes close to the original in meter as well as in meaning and was reprinted in England in 1842. In addition to Grandville's full-page engravings, vignettes and decorated initials adorn some of the English versions.

155 ———— THE FABLES OF LA FONTAINE, translated into English verse by Walter Thornbury. With three hundred illustrations by Gustave Doré, and one hundred etchings by famous French etchers. New York, Cassell [1873?] 2 v. 31 cm. PQ1811.E3T6

☆ The wood engravings of Doré appeared first in the French edition, *Fables de La Fontaine* (Paris, Hachette et Cie, 1868). In the full-page illustrations he creates a murky, sinister world with dark threatening landscapes of spacious proportion. The vignettes are lighter, more humorous. The only "famous French etcher" represented is the 18th-century Oudry, whose illustrations have an entirely different spirit, being much lighter and more relaxed. The jarring of the two styles is noticeable.

156 ———— FABLES. Éd. illustrée de 75 planches à l'eau-forte par A. Delierre. Paris, A. Quantin, 1883. 2 v. plates (part col.) 33 cm. PQ1808.A1 1883

☆ An elegant, expensive edition printed on heavy paper and illustrated with delicately engraved pastoral scenes, not humorous or original, but very pleasant—the trees especially. The title and half-title pages for each book are decorated with original watercolor drawings, usually of birds and plants, signed by Auguste Delierre and dated 1889, showing that they were added later. Classical borders surround the illustrations and many other ornaments adorn the book.

This edition was first published in 13 installments, from 1880 to 1883.

157 ——— THE FABLES OF JEAN DE LA FONTAINE, newly translated into English verse by Joseph Auslander and Jacques Le Clercq, with title-page and decorations engraved on copper by Rudolph Ruzicka. New York, The Limited Editions Club, 1930. 2 v. (266, 404 p.)

PQ1811.E3A8

An idiomatic translation, quite literal, in lively verse by two American poets, books 1–6 by Joseph Auslander and books 7–12 by Jacques Le Clercq. A short, witty introduction by Auslander gives some background for La Fontaine's life and the court of Louis XIV. Book 2 has a more ornate translation, as befits La Fontaine's originals, many of which are based on Eastern fables and stories. The Ruzicka decorations consist of a few lightly printed engravings. There are no notes or indications of sources.

158 ——— THE FABLES OF JEAN DE LA FONTAINE; translated into English verse by Edward Marsh; with twelve reproductions from engravings by Stephen Gooden. London, W. Heinemann, 1933. lxxi, 469 p. 22 cm.

PQ1811.E3M3 1933

Sir Edward Marsh's translations are witty and amusing. Monica Sutherland calls them "by far the best, though the Fables inevitably lose much in translation." This edition includes a translation of La Fontaine's preface and "Life of Aesop the Phrygian." An Everyman edition appeared in 1952 (London, Dent; New York, Dutton. No. 991) without the illustrations.

159 ——— SELECTED FABLES; translated by Eunice Clark; illustrated by Alexander Calder. New York, Quadrangle Press, 1948. 88 p. 32 cm.

PQ1811.E3C4

☆ Thirty-six fables in a lively, colloquial translation. The open, free line etchings of Calder are satirical and humorous in spirit. The book was reprinted in 1957 by George Braziller in a simpler binding.

160 ——— FABLES. Eaux-fortes originales de Marc Chagall. Paris, Tériade, 1952. 2 v. in 4. 39 cm.

PQ1808.A1 1952 Rosenwald Coll

☆ "Il a été tiré du présent ouvrage sur vélin de Rives quarante exemplaires comprenant cent eaux-fortes originales, peintes à la main par l'artiste. . . . Tous les exemplaires sont signés par l'artiste. Exemplaire numéro 33."

Stunning etchings with bright color—red, blue, yellow, or lavender—added by Chagall.

The portfolios include the text as well on pages of the same size,

Etching by Alexander Calder from La Fontaine's Selected Fables. *Copyright © 1948
by Quadrangle Press; reprinted by permission. The Man and the Wooden Idol.
(Item 159)*

printed in large, elegant type. A selection from the 100 etchings is
shown in the exhibition.

161 ——— THE FABLES OF LA FONTAINE; translated by Marianne Moore.
New York, Viking Press, 1954. `342 p.   PQ1811.E3M6   1954

☆   A free translation by the distinguished American poet preserves the
wit and wisdom of La Fontaine. With the fables themselves she has
translated the original dedication and preface. Jean Antoine Hou-
don's bust of La Fontaine is used as a frontispiece.
    The copy exhibited is No. 400 of the first edition, signed by the
translator.

162 ——— FABLES CHOISIES MISES EN VERS. [Introduction, notes et
relevé de variantes par Georges Couton] Paris, Garnier frères [1962]
xxxvii, 576 p.   PQ1808.A1   1962

    The introduction includes the history of fables before La Fontaine
and the story of the publication of his *Fables Choisies*. The text
contains his preface and "Vie d'Ésope" and the complete text of the
12 books. Comprehensive notes, p. 405–560, cover sources of the

fables, variations in text, and explanations of La Fontaine's use of archaic words.

The volume has a neat, modern format and is illustrated with reproductions of drawings, engravings, and tapestries from various sources.

Biographies and Studies

163 Rochambeau, Eugène Achille Lacroix de Vimeur, *comte* de. BIBLIO-GRAPHIE DES ŒUVRES DE LA FONTAINE. Paris, A. Rouquette, 1911. 699 p. illus. Z8470.6.R63

This invaluable reference book arranges the editions of La Fontaine's writings chronologically within the type of work: fables, contes, théâtre, *Psyché et Adonis*, œuvres diverses, and œuvres complètes—with fables of course taking most of the space—500 pages listing 2,059 editions.

The study gives complete bibliographical information for all editions in French. It includes also such books as *Phaedri, Augusti Liberti,* and collections of fables which contain some La Fontaine verses, single fables published separately, and those three that appeared in the *Mercure Galant* between 1690 and 1692.

In addition to the detailed descriptions of pagination, contents, etc., M. de Rochambeau provides interesting notes on variations in editions, indicating those which are taken from or are related to others and adding background information about the illustrations.

164 Taine, Hippolyte A. LA FONTAINE ET SES FABLES. 3. éd. Paris, L. Hachette, 1861. 351 p. PQ1812.T3 1861

In this critical study, first published in 1853, the noted French scholar and essayist shows sympathetic understanding and great knowledge of La Fontaine. He calls him France's Homer—"C'est La Fontaine qui est notre Homère" (p. 46)—because of the universality of his themes: men, gods, animals, landscapes, nature, and the society of the time. He interprets La Fontaine's fables as an accurate picture of the 17th century, from the lion king down to the plebian frogs and donkeys.

The first part, a short, anecdotal biography, offers general remarks on La Fontaine as a writer and as a type of "l'esprit gaulois." The second part contains a detailed analysis of the personages: men—the king and court, the courtesan, the nobility, monk, magistrate, merchant, and artisan; the beasts; and gods. The third part concerns La Fontaine's art, his style, and his inspiration from Aesop, Phaedrus, Rabelais, and Bidpai.

165 Saint-Marc Girardin, *known as.* LA FONTAINE ET LES FABULISTES. Paris, Michel Lévy frères, 1867. 2 v. (448, 484 p.) PQ1812.S3

This series of 28 lectures comprises a complete course on La Fontaine given by M. François Auguste Marc Girardin at the Sorbonne. As background, he traces the fable literature from Aesop, Phaedrus, and Babrius, from the oriental fables, and from those of the Middle Ages, including *Le Roman du Renard,* and compares La Fontaine to the earlier fabulists. He covers the character and life of La Fontaine and treats him as social critic, as philosopher, and as moralist. In conclusion he provides chapters on later French fabulists and on English and German writers in this genre.

166   Collins, William L. LA FONTAINE, AND OTHER FRENCH FABULISTS, by the Rev. W. Lucas Collins. Edinburgh, W. Blackwood, 1882. 176 p. (Foreign classics for English readers)   PQ1812.C6

A biographical and critical study of the French fabulist. The "Life of La Fontaine," p. 38–77, includes the traditional stories about his carelessness and incompetence; the rest of the book is concerned with commentary and critique on the fables themselves. Collins details the influence of the earlier French fable writers to whom La Fontaine was indebted and the *Reynard the Fox* stories. Short chapters discuss later fable writers Houdard de la Motte, Richter, Desbillions, Aubert, Monnier, Florian, and Le Bailly.

"La Fontaine has no claim to originality so far as his subject matter is concerned . . . it was by the charm of his style, and his mode of presenting them, that he made them virtually his own" (p. 15).

167   Lafenestre, Georges É. LA FONTAINE. Paris, Hachette, 1895. 207 p. (Les grands écrivains français)   PQ1812.L3

The first half of this delightful study relates the traditional legends concerning La Fontaine's life. The second part treats his works, his imagination and sensibility, his thought, style, and influence.

168   Hamel, Frank. JEAN DE LA FONTAINE. With photogravure frontispiece and sixteen other illustrations. New York, Brentano's, 1912. 389 p.   PQ1812.H3

☆   "List of chief authorities" (p. 15–16).

The standard biography in English, written in a popular style, although fully documented by research. Two chapters on the fables discuss many of them in detail, giving sources and following the course of the English translations through the mid-19th century.

169   Roche, Louis. LA VIE DE JEAN DE LA FONTAINE. Paris, Plon-Nourrit, 1913. 412 p.   NNUW

This readable, lively life of La Fontaine has been called "without doubt the most important contribution to the biography of the poet." Roche set out to fill the lacunae and even to correct errors in the earlier studies; his volume is well documented, with many footnotes which,

however, do not detract from its readability. He shows great understanding of La Fontaine as a person—both his lightness and his mel-
ancholy. In the chapter on "La Fontaine et les Philosophes" he
reveals how much La Fontaine had read and lists allusions to the
classical philosophers found in the fables.

170 Gohin, Ferdinand. L'ART DE LA FONTAINE DANS SES FABLES. Paris,
Garnier frères, 1929. 299 p. (Bibliothèque d'histoire littéraire et
de critique) PQ1808.G6

An important study treating La Fontaine's work as a whole, with
emphasis of course on the fables. Gohin analyzes the poetry, discussing the rhythms, the sonorities, and the rhymes used. He traces the
sources of some of the fables to obscure French writers as well as to
the fables of Barbrius, Phaedrus, and Avianus and shows how La
Fontaine changed some of the characters and often the point of view.

M. Gohin also edited a 2-volume edition of the *Fables de La
Fontaine* (Paris, Garnier, 1934).

171 Giraudoux, Jean. LES CINQ TENTATIONS DE LA FONTAINE (cinq con-
férences). Paris, B. Grasset [1938] 292 p. PQ1812.G5

The famous French author and playwright gives five original and
stimulating lectures on the life of La Fontaine, each a tableau of a
temptation of destiny against the life and spirit of La Fontaine.
These temptations are "de la vie bourgoise"; "des femmes"; "du
monde"; "la tentation littéraire"; and "la tentation du scepticisme et
de la religion."

To La Fontaine's fables only does the writer accord a major place
in literature. He studies the questions of the role of the moral and
of the "painter of the animals." At appropriate times in his lecture
programs he had actresses read from the fables and dedications.

172 Clarac, Pierre. LA FONTAINE, L'HOMME ET L'ŒUVRE. Paris, Boivin
[1947] 200 p. (Le Livre de l'étudiant, 21) PQ1812.C55

The author, Inspecteur Général de l'Éducation Nationale, has
edited several collections of La Fontaine's works. Here he sums up
modern studies of the fabulist. He notes that La Fontaine makes his
characters indviduals—each is a certain beast or man, not just a
symbol, as in earlier fables.

"Note bibliographique," p. [190]–200, is very helpful.

173 Sutherland, Monica (La Fontaine). LA FONTAINE. London, Cape
[1953] 192 p. PQ1812.S8

A straightforward biography based as much as possible on original
sources. At appropriate times the author discusses, with enthusiasm,
the best, most characteristic fables.

An appendix gives the location and importance of manuscripts and
letters. The selected bibliography, p. 189–190, is valuable.

174 La Fontaine, Jean de. LE PETIT LA FONTAINE. Paris, Marcilly [ca. 1835] 94 p. 4½ x 6½ cm. P1808.A2 1835 Min Case

☆ Book-plate: Wilbur Macey Stone.
A small book of 21 fables, with an illustrated title page pasted on its marbled paper cover and 6 other small engravings included.

175 —— QUELQUES FABLES. Paris, 1896. [61] p. 45 mm.
No. 159 Min Case

☆ A tiny book containing eight fables, without illustrations.

176 —— FABLES CHOISIES POUR LES ENFANTS et illustrées par M. B. de Monvel. Paris, Plon-Nourrit [n.d.] 48 p. 4PZ Fr.–2

☆ Each of these 24 familiar fables is illustrated with Maurice Boutet de Monvel's charming, delicate watercolors. The small pictures, several to a page, are full of character and humor.

177 —— THE FABLES OF LA FONTAINE; translated by Margaret Wise Brown, illustrations by André Hellé. New York, Harper [c1940] 39 p. 28½ x 22 cm. PZ8.2.L134Fp

☆ Illustrated lining-papers; title page illustrated in colors.
Smooth prose retellings for young children of 17 of the best-known fables. The illustrations by a French artist are simple, bright, and childlike.

178 —— FABLES DE LA FONTAINE. Illustrées par Simonne Baudoin. [Tournai] Casterman, [1955] 32 p. PQ1808.A2 1955

☆ A modern French picture book for young children, with large print and bright but soft colors. The same illustrations appear in the American edition, *The Fables of La Fontaine*, translated by Marie Ponsot (New York, Grosset & Dunlap [1957]).

179 —— THE LION AND THE RAT; a fable. Illustrated by Brian Wildsmith. New York, F. Watts [1963] [32] p. col. illus. 29 cm.
☆ PZ8.2.L134Wi2

180 —— THE NORTH WIND AND THE SUN; a fable. Illustrated by Brian Wildsmith. New York, F. Watts, 1964. [32] p. col. illus. 29 cm.
PZ8.2.L135No3

181 —— THE RICH MAN AND THE SHOEMAKER. Illustrated by Brian Wildsmith. New York, F. Watts, 1965. [32] p. col. illus. 29 cm.
PZ8.2.L136Ri4

These three beautiful picture books with their rich, glowing color and exuberant line and feeling stand out among the best examples of what can be done with a single tale.

Illustration by Brian Wildsmith from The Lion and the Rat. *Copyright © 1963 by Brian Wildsmith; reproduced by permission of Franklin Watts, Inc. (Item 179)*

Krylov

Drawing by David Pascal from 15 Fables of Krylov. Copyright © 1965 by David Pascal; reproduced by permission of the Macmillan Company. The Cat and the Starling. (Item 200)

KRYLOV

Krylov's sly, pointed, often cynical, tales are as well known to Russian children as La Fontaine is to the French schoolboy. Russian children are weaned on Krylov.

Ivan Andreevich Krylov was born on February 14, 1768, in Moscow. His father, a military officer, died when he was 11. In 1783 he moved with his mother to St. Petersburg, where he composed operas and tragedies without much success. After the death of his mother in 1788, he entered the public service for 2 years but resigned and brought out a journal, *The Spectator*. He again tried dramatic composition in 1800 and 1801. He acquired a taste for cards and as a young man played passionately.

Little is known about his private affairs. From 1806 on he led a simple life and worked as librarian at the St. Petersburg Public Library. His façade of an odd, simple, and lazy person protected him from the over-curious. He was very much aware of the political unrest—the uprisings, the Decembrists—of his times. After the reaction triumphed, Krylov was not reconciled to the existing social relationships but did not believe they would change. His later fables take on a more pessimistic note. Their political intent is very clear. Since it was the Czar who was in power at the time, it was he who bore the brunt of Krylov's wit.

The fables written from 1805 to 1808, the first of which were translations from La Fontaine, are in the normal fable spirit of mild social or personal criticism or pointing of a moral. Those written from 1813 to 1824 include more political satire, and those written from 1827 to 1834 are almost all political and social criticism. His world view did not change from a cynical look toward men and human institutions in general. He especially attacked hypocrisy, as well as general foolishness.

The first complete edition of Krylov's fables appeared in 1843, a year before his death. It contained 197 fables, the work of 30 years as a fable writer. His first attempt had been made about 1788 when he translated three of La Fontaine's fables while on vacation and was encouraged by his friends to try more. Some years he wrote nothing at all, as between 1824 and 1827; other years were extremely productive, such as 1814, 1818, and 1823, when he wrote as many as 20 a year.

Most recent Soviet biographers try to deny the fact that Krylov borrowed his themes or go to ludicrous lengths in an attempt to show "Krylov, the Russian" as an original artist, by derogating La Fontaine and spending pages on apology that Krylov borrowed his material. On the other hand, Krylov's genius is not appreciated in the Western world to the extent which it deserves. There is no full-length biography in English, and none appears to be available in French or German.

Editions of the Fables

182 Krylov, Ivan A. Novyia basni. Saint Petersburg, County Government, 1811. 41 p. 20 cm. PG3337.K7B3 1811 Rare Bk

   The earliest edition owned by the Library of Congress is this first
edition of the 21 fables of the third book, without illustrations.

183 ——— Basni. Saint Petersburg, Publishing House of the State Sen-
ate, 1815. 47, 41, 41 p. PG3337.K7B3 1815 Rare Bk

   Bound with volume 2 of the author's *Basni* (Saint Petersburg, 1819).
Many engraved plates by I. A. Ivanov show classical figures of gods
and people as well as animals.

184 ——— Basni v semi knigakh. New, corrected, and augmented ed.
Saint Petersburg, I. Slenin, 1825. 312 p.
PG3337.K7B3 1825 Rare Bk

☆   An expensive, elegant edition, with green tooled morocco cover,
this contains the first seven books. The plates by I. A. Ivanov, one for
each book, are not the same as those in the 1815 edition.

185 ——— Fables russes, tirées du recueil de M. Kriloff, et imitées en
vers français et italiens, par divers auteurs; précédées d'une introduc-
tion française de M. Lemontey, et d'une préface italienne de M. Salfi.
Publiées par M. le comte Orloff. Ornées du portrait de M. Kriloff.
Paris, Bossange, 1825. 2 v. (lxi, 249, 381 p.) plates.
PG3337.K7B345

☆   The 86 Krylov fables were translated by 88 poets. The introduction says that M. le comte Orloff began by translating into French
prose, as literal as possible, the fables of his compatriot; this material
was put at the disposal of French and Italian poets who, "avec la
liberté du talent," made verses out of Orloff's translation.

   After comparing the Russian language with other European languages, Lemontey discusses the three Russian fabulists Khemnitzer,
Dmitrief, and Krylov.

186 ——— Fables de M. J. Krylof. Traduites du Russe, d'après l'édition complète de 1825. Par Hippolyte Masclet. Moscow, de
l'Imprimerie d'Auguste Semen, 1828. 270 p.
PG3337.K7B345 1828

   Already in 1828 dissatisfaction with Count Orloff's edition, as not
being literal enough or giving any feeling for the Russian, led
Masclet to make a more literal translation of the first seven books.

187 ——— Basni. Saint Petersburg. A. Smyrdin, 1834. 2 v. (187,
167, xx p.) 26 cm. PG3337.K7B3 1834

☆ A well-known edition of seven books, with many humorous drawings by A. P. Sapozhnikov, caricaturing people and animals.

188 —— BASNI V VOS'MI KNIGAKH. Saint Petersburg, A. A. Pliushara,
1840. 300 p. port. PG3337.K7B3

☆ An edition which includes eight of Krylov's nine books of fables.
Most of the half-page engravings, signed by J. J. Grandville, are
those made for La Fontaine's fables in 1838. The illustrations for
original Krylov fables are in the same style.

189 —— BASNI V DEV'TI KNIGAKH. Saint Petersburg, Military Educa-
tion Publishing House, 1843. 326 p. 23 cm.
PG3337.K7B3 1843 Yudin Coll

The first complete edition, containing all nine books (book 9 has
only 11 fables). The Library of Congress copy is in poor condition,
its soft paper having been torn. It has no notes or illustrations.

190 —— BASNI. Saint Petersburg, Government Publications Clearing-
house, 1856. 86 p. port. 30 mm. PG3337.K7B3 1856 Min Case

☆ The smallest edition of the fables; one literally needs a magnifying
glass to read it. It has been bound in vellum, with medallions on the
covers, and is in a leather slipcase. The Library of Congress keeps it
in a tiny box.

191 —— ORIGINAL FABLES. Translated by I. Henry Harrison. London, Remington, 1883. xxxii, 228 p. PG3337.K7B34

Harrison translated, in verse, 142 of the original fables, omitting
22. Of Krylov's 38 borrowed fables, Harrison translated 7 as specimens
of his treatment.

He lists the fables chronologically, indicating those which are original, those borrowed, and the sources of the borrowed fables. An introduction gives a short account of Krylov's life mentioning his translations of La Fontaine, which led him to original composition in the
same style. Later learning Greek, he took some fables direct from
Aesop.

Harrison says in the introduction (p. xxxii), "Kriloff is beyond all
question as national as he is original, and he is the crowned king of
the fabulists of all languages."

192 —— BASNI KRYLOVA. Nolnoe so'ranie. Izdanie tret'e. Moscow,
A. IA. Panafidin, 1900. 302, [10] p. 11 cm.
PG3337.K7B3 1900 Rare Bk

☆ A little book, containing the full collection of the fables, with 75
full-page illustrations, plus many smaller ones, by N. V. Denisov.
This copy comes from the classroom of the younger princesses in the
Alexandrovsky Palace, and the flyleaf is inscribed: Olga, Tatiana,
Maria, Anastasia.

193 ——— Krilòff's fables; translated from the Russian into English into the orginal metres, by C. Fillingham Coxwell. With 4 plates. London, K. Paul, Trench, Trubner; New York, Dutton [1920] 176 p.

PG3337.K7B34 1920

Coxwell translated 86 of Krylov's fables "as closely as possible to the original Russian." The result is long and elaborate, with many inverted sentences. He did not translate all the morals but has notes on their probable political meanings. His long introduction (p. 1–37) includes biographical information, with anecdotes, and evaluation of Krylov's fables in relation to the traditional ones and to La Fontaine's, and his place in Russian literature as "the first national poet."

"It was said in Russia that Kriloff's spirit was unrecognisable in the French and Italian translations made at the instance of Count Orloff in 1825" (p. 29).

194 ——— Krylov's Fables, translated into English verse with a preface by Bernard Pares. New York, Harcourt, Brace [1927] 271 p.

PG3337.K7B34 1927

A good modern translation, both literal and lively, by an English scholar who was a professor of Russian at London University. It was issued in paperback in 1942 by Penguin Books (Middlesex, Eng., and New York), with the English and Russian on opposite pages, numbered in duplicate (PG3337.K7R8).

195 ——— Basni. Moscow, Academy of Sciences, U.S.S.R., 1956. 635 p.

PG3337.K7B3 1956

A complete edition of Krylov's fables which aims to be definitive. The commentary section by A. P. Mogilianskii has notes on each fable, giving sources and variants, and a line-by-line analysis of the different phraseology found in the different editions (about 3,000 lines in the 201 fables). Lists of the dates of composition and first publication of all the fables are included, preceding the index. The plates reproduce examples of illustrations from various editions.

Biographies and Studies

196 Kenevich, Vladislav. I. A. Krylov: Bibliograficheskīā i istoricheskīā primiechanīā k basniam Krylova. 2 v. Saint Petersburg, 1878. 392 p.

PGR1521.A4K3 1878

This early study contains biographical and historical remarks on the fables of Krylov with materials for his biography. Later biographies are based on it.

197 Stepanov, Nikolai L. I. A. KRYLOV; ZHIZN I TVORCHESTVO. Moscow, State Publishing House of Art-Literature, 1958. 467 p. port.

PG3337.K7Z932

A study of Krylov's life and creative activity, based on two of the author's earlier works, a biography of Krylov (Moscow, 1949), and a study of the fables (Moscow, 1956). In discussing Krylov's growth as a fable writer, Stepanov emphasizes the political nature of the later fables. As Krylov's style and world view matured, his fables took on a more pessimistic note, and those written from 1827 to 1834 are almost all political satires directed against existing social relationships.

Editions for Children

198 Krylov, Ivan A. KRILOF AND HIS FABLES, by W. R. S. Ralston. London, Strahan, 1869. 180 p. illus. PZ8.2.K95Kr

A literal prose translation of about half of Krylov's fables, with a preface by Ralston giving biographical information.

199 ———— BASNI. Moscow, State Publishing House of Art-Literature, 1947. 109 p. 27 cm. PG3337.K7B3 1947

☆ A typical Soviet children's edition, containing 25 fables illustrated in 4 distinct and very different styles (wood engraving, silhouettes, and drawings).

200 ———— 15 FABLES OF KRYLOV. Translated by Guy Daniels. Illustrated by David Pascal. New York, Macmillan [c1965] 33 p. 26 cm. PZ8.2.K95Fi

☆ A fine idiomatic translation in rhymed verse, which has kept close to the Russian original. The full-page illustrations, black-and-white pen drawings with swift, flowing lines, caricature people and animals and are full of satiric humor.

U.S. GOVERNMENT PRINTING OFFICE: 1966   O—792-502

www.ingramcontent.com/pod-product-compliance
Lightning Source LLC
Chambersburg PA
CBHW030538180626
46810CB00005B/1927